P9-EKD-843

MAVERICK BASIN

OTHER FIVE STAR WESTERNS BY DANE COOLIDGE:

Man from Wyoming (2000)
The Wild Bunch (2003)
Bitter Creek (2004)
Snake Dance (2005)
The Soldier's Way (2006)
Rider of Death Valley (2008)

MAVERICK BASIN

A WESTERN STORY

DANE COOLIDGE

FIVE STAR

A part of Gale, Cengage Learning

Detroit • New York • San Francisco • New Haven, Conn • Waterville, Maine • London

0|09, 11

GALE
CENGAGE Learning

Copyright © 2009 by Golden West Literary Agency.
The Acknowledgments on page 197 constitute an extension of the copyright page.
Five Star Publishing, a part of Gale, Cengage Learning.

LIBRARY OF CONGRESS CATALOGING-IN-PUBLICATION DATA

Coolidge, Dane, 1873–1940.
    Maverick Basin : a western story / by Dane Coolidge. — 1st ed.
        p. cm.
        ISBN-13: 978-1-59414-818-7 (alk. paper)
        ISBN-10: 1-59414-818-X (alk. paper)
        I. Title.
PS3505.O5697M38 2009
813'.52—dc22   2009001229

First Edition. First Printing: May 2009.
Published in 2009 in conjunction with Golden West Literary Agency.

Printed in the United States of America
1 2 3 4 5 6 7 13 12 11 10 09

MAVERICK BASIN

CHAPTER ONE

There was a hush, a boding silence in Deadman Cañon, and skirling hawks, flying high against the cliffs, settled down and watched expectantly. A man was riding warily up the Maverick Basin trail, and ahead, like hunting animals, two men were skulking forth to cut him off at the creek. Above them, stuck tightly as mud wasps' nests to the shelves of sun-blackened crags, the white houses of cliff-dwellers, now desolate and tenantless, gazed down upon the age-old tragedy, but the man rode on, his rifle beneath his knee, and at the stalking place of the Scarboroughs he stopped. A stream of cold water, gushing out of a deep side chasm, formed a swirl in the tepid waters of the creek, and close to its edge a flat stone had been laid, where a man could kneel and drink. He knelt, and, when he rose up, he was looking down a gun.

"Put 'em up!" commanded a voice.

He started back defiantly, at which a second voice came from the side.

"Right quick!" it added.

As the stranger obeyed, Isham Scarborough stepped out from behind his rock. He was tall and slim, as befitted a Texan, with a red, freckled face, lips swollen by the sun, and eyelashes bleached yellowish-white. A huge, black hat made him tower like a giant as he glowered down insolently upon his captive, and, after a long, searching look, he jabbed him in the ribs and reached out to take his gun. But the stranger stepped away with

7

waspish quickness and at the look in his eyes Isham flinched and drew back while his brother rose up to shoot. Red Scarborough was short and chunky, with flaming red hair and eyes with a piggish glint, and, when he shouted out a warning, the stranger's hands shot up, for he, too, had learned to read eyes. Red strode forth wrathfully and twitched away the prisoner's gun, then whirled on the startled Isham.

"You're going to get killed," he warned, "if you don't quit monkeying with these fellers."

"Huh, huh," scoffed Isham, and swaggered up to the man, regarding him with his head to one side. "You're bad, now, ain't ye?" he demanded. "Well, we'll soon break you of that. Where d'ye think you're going with that horse?"

The stranger blinked and regarded him intently, then drew down his lips to a line. He was dark and slender, with flashing black eyes and the high cheek bones of a fighter, but now he was ominously calm.

"I am going," he said, "to Maverick Basin. Is this a hold-up, or what?"

"It's a hold-up," replied Isham, "and you're dad-burned lucky it didn't turn out a killing. I had my six-shooter on your heart, and, if you'd ever went for that gun . . . we'd've left you here for the buzzards. What takes you over into Maverick Basin?"

"That's my business," replied the prisoner, suddenly matching Isham's arrogance.

Isham glanced meaningly at his brother. "Oh, it is, eh?" he observed, reaching over behind a rock and fetching out a rawhide rope. "Well, I'll damned soon show you that it's mine!"

He shook out a loop, flipped it back into the sand, and then, with the practiced skill of a cowboy, snapped it over his prisoner's head. Before he could move, the stranger's arms were pinioned, and, as the rope was jerked taut, Red caught him from behind and tied his hands, hard and fast.

"Now," cursed Red, "come through, Mister Man . . . are you going in to join them sorry Blacks?"

"Never heard of 'em," answered the man, and Red's sunburned lips drew back in a hateful, distorted grin.

"I know that's a lie," he said, "so we'll jest cut you off right here."

He motioned to Isham, and, with their prisoner between them, they toiled up a trail to the east. The cañon wall was low on that side of the creek and at the base of the cliff there was a row of cliff-dwellings, strung along under the overhang of the rim.

It was from behind their loopholed walls that the Scarboroughs watched the trail, to cut off such chance travelers as he was, and, as the prisoner climbed up, his lip curled scornfully at the sight of their elaborate precautions. In spite of their bluster something still seemed to tell him that they were not as bad as they looked, although often, as he knew, the most hideous crimes have been committed by cravens at heart. They entered a low door and passed on from room to room until at last he was thrust into a dark and noisome space and bound with his back against a post.

It was one of those black holes that the cliff-dwellers themselves had apparently used as a prison and against the square of light that poured in from above he saw the heavy lattice of bars. Wooden bars, and something else—and, as he looked again, he saw the sinister outlines of a loop. It hung from a beam like the slack body of a snake, and there was a hangman's knot on the end.

"Now," began Isham Scarborough, "perhaps you can talk. You ain't the first sorry horse thief that has tried to hold out on us, but they danged sure talked . . . or hung. So you never even heard of the sorry Blacks?"

"No, I never did," answered the prisoner stoutly, and Isham

shook down the loop.

"Say, now, listen," he warned, "we know dog-goned well that you ain't no friend of ours. We're from Texas, see, and back where we come from no white man rides a saddle like that. So you're ditched at the start by that center-fire rigging and the danged fresh way you've got, but before we stretch your neck, we'll give you a chance to tell where you got that horse."

He paused and opened up the hangman's loop, and the prisoner found his tongue.

"I bought him in Bowie," he declared in a passion, "and I've got the bill of sale in my pocket. But I swear I never heard of the Blacks in my life . . . and I don't know what you're talking about."

"Well, the Bassett gang, then," broke in Red Scarborough roughly, "ain't you never heerd tell of the dirty, black Bassetts? Well, that's the outfit we're talking about."

"Well, why didn't you say so?" demanded the prisoner resentfully. "Of course I've heard of the Bassetts. But is that any reason for holding a man up and threatening to hang him for a horse thief? You must be some of the Scarboroughs, but they informed me back in Tonto. . . ."

"And what did they inform you?" prompted Isham hectoringly, and the prisoner drew himself up.

"I was informed," he said, "that the Scarboroughs were Southern gentlemen."

"*Uhr*," jeered Red.

"Well?" Isham inquired.

"And as a Southerner myself . . . ," began the prisoner.

Isham cut him off short. "You ignorant, black rascal," he burst out in a fury, "don't you dare to open your mouth and say a word ag'in' the Scarboroughs or I'll kick your dog-goned head off. You've got Injun blood yourse'f, if I'm any judge, and I know for a certainty you're going into the basin to throw in with them dirty, black Bassetts!"

"No, you're mistaken," answered the prisoner firmly. "I'm just looking for a certain party that I know."

"Oho," exclaimed Red, stooping to feel for his badge, "so we've picked up an officer, have we?"

"No, again," replied the prisoner. "I am looking for a friend, and your quarrels are nothing to me."

"Well, *er* . . . who is this friend?" inquired Isham suspiciously, but the stranger shook his head.

"I can't tell you that, but I give you my word of honor I am not going in to join the Bassetts. And now, if you'll kindly untie these ropes. . . ."

"Don't you think it," raged Isham, "not after what you did! You murdering black hound, you started to grab your gun and gut-shoot me before I could pull. You're a Bassett gunman and you'll never git past here, so you might as well say your prayers. Come on, Red, let's string him up."

"Naw, let him wait," answered Red impatiently. "I want to keep my eye on that trail. Let's git that other jasper and throw him in here, too, and then, if they don't come through, we can hang 'em both."

They withdrew hurriedly, and, as he listened to their footsteps, the prisoner ventured the ghost of a smile. It was very impressive, with the hangman's knot and all, but in spite of their bluster he still doubted their big words and their threats to take his life. As for this other prisoner—he dismissed him with a shrug and turned to inspect his cell. But as he gazed at the blank walls, he heard a scuffle without and the *thud* of heavy blows, and then a hoarse voice burst out in frightful oaths that were smothered as the struggles increased.

"You ain't man enough!" it roared, suddenly blaring out again. "No, you can't put me in there, the two of you!"

There was a rush and a slapping of feet, choking curses, and a chorus of grunts, and then Isham plunged through the doorway, heaving away at a rope, while his brother fought the prisoner from behind. The rope, which had once been thrown about the prisoner's neck, was clutched back by a huge, hairy hand, and, as Red pushed him in, the other hand swept out in a last, bear-like swipe at his head. But the Scarboroughs were powerful men, accustomed to roping and tying steers, and despite his efforts they dragged him to a post and tied his hands together behind it.

"Oh, we cain't, hey?" Isham taunted, and the new prisoner panted angrily as he shook back his tumbled black hair.

"You danged, ornery cow thieves," he began in measured tones, "I know what's the matter with you. You're jealous. You want all the stealing for yourselves. You ain't satisfied with taking what comes your way. You want to hog it all. But I'll see you in hell first, you low-down Texican polecats, before I'll. . . ."

"Shut up!" broke in Isham, giving him a boot in the ribs, and, as he burst out in wicked curses, they crawled out the doorway and closed it with a huge flat stone. There was a hush as their footsteps clumped away into silence, and then, beneath the shadow of the hangman's knot, the prisoners sat and stared at each other.

CHAPTER TWO

The man trap of the Scarboroughs had caught a wampus when it snared this second rider of the trails. He was huge, and bearded like Olympian Zeus—a black, curling beard that stood out in bunches beneath strands of long, tousled hair. His nose was small and snubbed, his mouth a cavern of noise, and the rolling blue eyes revealed a depth of ferocity that put him near to a brute, yet, as he gazed at his fellow prisoner, the savagery fell away from him and his smile was almost human.

"Hello there, pardner," he greeted with a nod, "so they've got you in here, too. Well, by grab, I never thought, after all I been through, to git caught with a bait like that, but when I sees that rock, I piles off my horse and drops down to git me a drink, and I'll be shot if Isham Scarborough wasn't right behind that boulder with his Winchester ready to shoot. I surrendered. I had to, or the dirty Texas cowards would have killed me like beefing a steer. But you wait till I git out of here, and, if I don't lift their hair, my name ain't Meshackatee, that's all. I'll throw in with 'em if I have to . . . because the Bassetts are no better and I don't aim to die by hanging . . . but it's gitting pretty rank when a man can't ride this cañon without being roped and tied. How'd they work it to pick you up?"

"The same way they caught you," confessed the other. "I got down to take a drink, and, when I looked up, I was covered. If there hadn't been two of them. . . ."

"Yes"—Meshackatee nodded—"I know how you feel. I

reckon you're a man of some nerve. But them boys would've killed you without batting an eye. By the way, what'd you say your name was?"

"My name is Hall," replied the stranger after a silence, and the giant bowed to him gravely.

"Glad to meet you, Hall," he responded cordially. "You might've heard of Meshackatee? No? Well, that's the name I go by, the same as yours is Hall. I got it among the Apaches. Wahoo Meshackatee. But some ignorant old wallopers still insist on calling me Jinglebob. Name I had in New Mexico . . . got mixed up in a range war . . . but out here they all call me Meshackatee. Kind of an Injun name or maybe it's Irish. The circumstances was something like this.

"I got run out of New Mexico . . . or maybe I moved . . . anyhow, I come away, dragging my tracks out behind me, and I butted right into some cavalry. They was out trailing Injuns . . . a bunch of Apaches that had left the reservation on a raid . . . and the lieutenant in command, seeing that my hair was kinder long, inquires if I could talk Apache. Well, to tell you the truth now, I couldn't speak a word of it, but in order to git my teeth into some of that Army grub, I told him I could *habla* it fine. He took me on as scout and Injun interpreter at five dollars a day and found, but at the end of two days we ran spang into them Injuns, and the lieutenant, he sent me out.

"Well, I rode up on a hill where they could see me good and held up my hand for a talk, and, when the old chief and a couple of bucks rode out, I hollers . . . 'Wahoo meshackatee!'

"The old chief, then, he rears back on his haunches and cuts loose with a bunch of Apache, and finally the lieutenant, who was fresh from West Point, rides up and asks what he says. Well, it was up to me then to make good or bust, so, knowing the dirty bastards, I made a bold guess and, by grab, it turned out I was right. 'He says, sir,' I reports, 'that his men want to fight,

14

but if you'll give him some grub, and some coffee and tobacco smokum, they'll think about coming in.'

"Well, we brought up the grub and the tobacco smokum, and, when them bucks saw it, they laid down their guns and come into camp on the lope. I was a hero, by cracky, until we got back to San Carlos and rustled up a real interpreter, but the colonel was so tickled that he kept me on the payroll under the name of Wahoo Meshackatee. Never could speak the lingo but them Apaches all know me and we git along somehow, by signs. But, say, where you going . . . on your way to join the Bassetts . . . or was you jest passing through?"

"No, I was just passing through," answered Hall uneasily, "and, by the way, who are these men, anyway? I'm a stranger in this country and I can't make out yet why they take so much interest in my business."

"Who . . . these fellers? Why, them's Isham and Red John Scarborough, two of the dangedest cow thieves unhung, and, as I told 'em just now, they're jealous. There's three brothers of 'em, altogether, and three of the Bassetts, and they used to be hand in glove. They throwed in together to steal old Jensen blind, but now it's dog eat dog. The Bassetts are part Injun and don't want no trouble, but these biggoty Texicans are crowding 'em so hard that I look for the fireworks any time. The Scarboroughs are hiring gunmen . . . you might git a job yourself . . . and fixing to run the Bassetts out of the country, and the Bassetts, for revenge, are going to bring in some sheep, and that sure will start a war. They're just watching each other now, and guarding the trails, but there ain't no use of your trying to git in there unless you join one of the gangs. If these boys'd let you pass, the Bassetts would sure git you, and so on, plumb through the basin. It's all split up, and I favor the Bassetts, but under the circumstances, and considering how we're fixed, I think we'd better join the Scarboroughs."

He glanced up at the loop of the hangman's knot and winked with a knowing leer, but the back of the other prisoner suddenly straightened against the post and fire flashed up in his eyes.

"What, join these men after they've held me up and accused me of being a horse thief? I'd die first. I'd let them hang me, before I'd even consider it. They're nothing but a pair of criminals!"

"Well, suit yourself," observed Meshackatee, glancing uneasily toward the door, "but you don't need to holler quite so loud."

"I'll say it to their faces!" cried Hall in a passion. "They're a disgrace to the name of Southerners. I'm from the South myself, and back in Kentucky a man holds his honor above his life. Do you think I'll submit to being branded a horse thief and not call them out, if I live?"

"From Kentucky, eh?" Meshackatee grinned. "Well, this is Arizona, a whole lot farther west, and over in the basin, where they're all from Uvalde, the term horse thief is jest a pet name."

"Uvalde?" repeated Hall. "I don't quite understand you."

"Uvalde University! Didn't you ever hear of Uvalde? That's a school for Texas cow thieves. The teacher in this college is an old, busted-down cowpuncher that's spent half his life in the pen, and his schoolhouse is a corral full of dust. He starts them boys off at drawing brands in the dirt, and then he puts 'em to work altering 'em, and, when a boy can burn every cow brand in Texas, he sends him out here with his diplomy. The diplomy? Oh, that's jest one of these here running irons to use on his neighbor's cows."

"Yes, I see," responded Hall, smiling absently and falling into a ruminative silence. "Is it a fact," he asked at last, "that over in Maverick Basin the people are as desperate as you say? I can understand this feud but I can't conceive of a community where a man will let you call him a thief."

"Well, they're Texicans, you know," explained Meshackatee glibly, "ain't supposed to have no morals, nohow. They're a cowardly bunch, too . . . jest look how they roped me . . . I never did see but one brave one. He's dead now, the rascal, but they called him One-Eyed Tex. I was there when he got his name. It was over in New Mexico and he got into a shooting scrape and the other feller plugged him through the eye. Bullet went plumb through his head and blew out part of his brains . . . made him feel kinder dizzy for a spell. Then he come to himself and drilled his man dead center, after which they took him to the doctor. The doctor wouldn't touch him till they told him it was Tex, and then he sewed him right up. Said a feller from Texas never would miss his brains nohow and he'd heal up and grow hair in a week.

"Well, Tex, he got well, and I will say for him that there was one sure enough brave Texan. He'd take on anybody and give 'em the first two shots and git off for self-defense. He come on over to Bowie, or I believe it was Lordsburg, but anyway his reputation had preceded him. He was known to be bad, and he shore run it over them Mexicans. You couldn't kill the scoundrel and there warn't no way to stop him, until some of them rawhides chopped his head plumb off one night and hid it out in the brush. He starved to death in about a week. But there was one brave Texican."

"But he's dead, eh?" Hall grinned, and then they both laughed while Meshackatee leered at the door.

"Ever spent much time exploring these cliff-dwellings?" he inquired, suddenly changing the subject. "Well, they sure are an interesting study. Supposed to have been built about a thousand years ago by the ancestors of the Aztecs or the Hopis, but let me tell you, pardner, they ain't all vanished yet. I found some, up here in a cave. I was riding along one time when I seen an old man, with his beard plumb down to his knees, and he was sitting down outside of a cliff-dwelling and crying like his heart would break.

" 'What's the matter, old man?' I says, and he bursts out worse than ever.

" 'My daddy whipped me!' he says, and I seen right there he was touched. He was a hundred years old if he was a day and his backbone was sticking through like a fish's, and of course he didn't have no daddy, but I was kind of sorry, the way he took on, and I gits down and pats him on the head.

" 'Well, don't cry,' I says, 'what did he whip you for?'

" 'Fer throwing stones at Grandpap,' he says, and cries like his heart would break.

" '*Aw,* hell,' I says, 'you ain't got no grandpap.'

" 'Yes I have!' he sobs. 'He's right up in that house!' And he points to one of these dwellings.

" 'Well, don't cry,' I says, 'mebbe I can fix it up for you. Is your daddy up there, too?'

" 'Yes,' he says, 'he's in that first room, gitting ready to trim his corns.'

"Well, of course I knowed he didn't have no dad . . . or at least it didn't seem possible . . . but jest to snoop into things and git to look around I went up the trail to the house. It was one jest like this, with the doors and windows sealed, but when I looked in, there was an old, old man, sharpening a butcher knife across his shin. He was so old and dried up there warn't no skin on his shin bone and his back was bent plumb to his knees. By grab, I was skeered . . . it didn't look natural . . . but of course I never let on.

" 'Hello!' I says, 'what are you whipping your kid for? He's down there crying his heart out.'

" 'Well, I don't keer,' he says, 'he's got to quit pestering his grandpap. The old man is gitting feeble and don't like to be disturbed, and that boy is always pelting him with stones.'

" 'Where is the old man?' I asks at last, and he points to a room in behind.

"It was one jest like this . . . you couldn't hardly see and it smelled kind of dead-like and close . . . and, when I looked around, I couldn't find nothing but an old, dried-up bundle of bones. Well, I tiptoed my way out of there and I says to the old-timer . . . the one that was trimming his corns . . . 'Your father ain't alive . . . he's dead!'

" 'No, he ain't,' he says, 'he only seems that way. But you take him down and throw him into the crick and let him soak for a while and he'll tell you about things that happened a thousand years ago!' "

Meshackatee threw back his head and joined in the laugh that followed his chef-*d'oeuvre,* and then he leaned over and nodded at Hall while he took him into confidence with a wink.

"On the level, now," he said, "ain't you an officer of the law? You've sure got that manhunter look. No? Nothing like that? Well, all right then, I'll quit guessing . . . you was going in to join the Bassetts."

He nodded again, wisely, but the stranger shook his head and tugged at his bonds impatiently.

"No," he said, "I never heard of the Bassetts till I asked about the basin in Tonto. And I never heard of the Scarboroughs until the livery stable keeper recommended them highly as Southern gentlemen. It appears he was mistaken, for I never met men yet who were their match for out-and-out insolence, but did it ever occur to you that a man might be going through here on business that concerned no one but himself? You have been connected with the Bassetts, and the Scarboroughs have trapped you . . . very well, join whichever side you will. But I for one will never join either, for I know what these family feuds lead to. I have seen whole counties plunged into a war that has lasted

Dane Coolidge

for twenty years. I have seen brave men . . . yes, and women and children, too . . . shot down and their murderers go unpunished. I left my own home to escape just such conditions as these Scarboroughs are trying to bring on, and, without professing any knowledge of the rights of the matter, I maintain that both sides are wrong. Whatever their differences they should endeavor to reconcile them before things have gone too far, for after the first shot, after the first man has been killed, his blood will cry out for more. Then brother must avenge brother and fathers their sons, and so on forever, as far as I know, or until God performs some miracle. And you, my friend, if you take my advice, will withdraw from this quarrel now, because after the first bloodshed it will be too late . . . you cannot desert your friends. I know whereof I speak, for I come from Kentucky where there is never an end to these wars, and so I entreat you, for you seem a good man, to flee from this feud while you can."

"For cripes' sake," muttered Meshackatee, "we must have caught a preacher." And then he raised his voice. "It's all right, boys!" he bellowed. "Come on in and turn us loose. He's nothing but a Christian gentleman."

The stone against the doorway was thrown back with a *thud* and the Scarboroughs stepped in again, grinning.

CHAPTER THREE

It was the evident purpose of the Scarboroughs to gloss over their misdemeanors by an affectation of jovial good humor, but the victim of the jest sat back with narrowed eyes while he glanced from them to Meshackatee.

"Oh, I see," he said with a mirthless smile, "this is supposed to be a joke."

"That's the idea," responded Meshackatee, "but it didn't work out. We thought all the time you was a Bassett."

"And if I had been?" inquired Hall.

Isham looked up from where he was untying the ropes. "We'd've stretched your damned neck," he replied succinctly. "Plain shooting is too good for them rascals."

"And what now?" went on the stranger. "Do I get my horse back, with an apology for all this rough treatment, or must I . . . ?"

"You do not!" returned Isham. "We don't apologize to nobody. You're lucky to git off alive."

"Very well," answered Hall, and the tone of his voice suggested reprisals to come.

"What d'ye mean?" flared up Isham. "You're pretty danged fresh for a man that's jest saved his neck."

"Perhaps so," he assented. "Am I still your prisoner, or am I free to go?"

"You'll wait until I ask you a few more questions." And Isham beckoned his brother to one side. They talked together with

21

their eyes on their prisoner, and then Isham Scarborough returned. Although he was the leader of the gang, both Red and Meshackatee seemed to regard him with scant respect; yet he was their spokesman, being by nature loud and boastful, while Red was watchful and silent, and he began with some general remarks.

"Now lookee here, my friend," he said, stepping closer and looking his prisoner in the eye, "you don't want to think, jest because you're bad, that anybody around here's afraid of you. The *hombre* don't live that can make me apologize, and you'd better not make any threats. But if you'll answer a few questions and act like a gentleman, we'll let you go into the basin. Now, who is this feller that you're looking for so hard . . . and does he belong to the Bassetts or the Scarboroughs?"

"Not to either, that I know of. He may not be in the basin, but I give you my word that this mission of mine has nothing to do with your quarrel."

"Yes, but what's his name?" persisted Isham shrewdly. "If we knowed who he was, we could danged soon find out for you. . . ."

"I cannot give his name," answered the stranger firmly, and Isham reared up his head.

"*Aw*, let 'im go on," broke in Red John impatiently. "But, say, what about that horse?"

"Well, make your own talk," replied Isham sulkily, and Red came over with a grin.

"That's all right, pardner," he said. "Sorry to make you any trouble, but we've got to keep watch of these trails. Now about that horse. He's got a New Mexico brand on him and that's liable to git you into trouble. But I've got a big bay that everybody knows, and jest to ride him will git you by anywhere. I'll trade you the bay and ten dollars to boot. . . ."

"No, I'm sorry," returned Hall, "but my horse is a pet and I couldn't consider a trade."

"Give you twenty-five dollars!" urged Red John eagerly, but the stranger shook his head.

"No," he said. "And now can I go?"

"You can go," spoke up Isham, "but I'll have to send along a guide to protect you against the Bassetts. Because if they ketch you now, after you've been stopping with us. . . ."

"I can protect myself," answered the stranger shortly, and Red broke into a laugh.

"Why didn't you do it, then?" he taunted, "when we nabbed you by the spring? I reckon you're pretty green in these parts."

"Yes, I'm green," admitted Hall, "but I'm beginning to learn . . . and I'm willing to take a chance on the Bassetts."

"Oh, you think they ain't so bad, eh?" broke in Isham intolerantly. "Well, let me tell you a few things about the Bassetts. They're a cross between a horse thief and a Digger Injun squaw, and they's more than one man that's dropped suddenly out of sight while he was riding across their range. They're the most treacherous bastards that ever was born and them that knows 'em best trusts 'em least. They're jest naturally bad with a yaller stripe down their belly as broad as the flat of your hand. They'll do everything but fight, and you can't crowd 'em to it . . . not if you call 'em every name you can lay your tongue to. And they're the orneriest-looking rascals that a white man ever seen . . . like an Injun, but black as niggers. You ain't going to throw in with an outfit like that . . . and call yourself a Southerner?"

"Whoever said I was going to throw in with them?" demanded Hall with outraged dignity. "Haven't I told you distinctly that I am just going through the country and that I don't give a damn about your quarrel?"

"Yes, you've told me," retorted Isham, "but perhaps I don't believe you. I wasn't born yesterday, and, if you don't want to join them, why do you object to going in with Meshackatee?"

"I don't object!" replied the prisoner tartly, "and, if that's a condition, I agree to it. But since my word of honor means nothing to you gentlemen, I must ask permission to withdraw it."

"Why, sure," mocked Isham, bowing low and with a smirk. "By grab, boys, we've sure caught a preacher."

"Nope, he ain't no preacher," corrected Meshackatee grimly. "And say, if we're going, let's start."

"Take him over to the Rock House, then," ordered Isham gruffly, "and don't let him git away."

"Very well, sir," answered Meshackatee, and with a half-mocking salute he led his prisoner away.

They were well up the trail before either of them spoke and then Meshackatee broke the silence.

"I'll take your word of honor," he said, "that you won't try to quit me on the trail. They'll hold me responsible now."

"You have it," replied Hall at length, "but I must say I'm surprised to find a man like you in the company of such unprincipled hounds."

"Oh, they ain't so bad," responded Meshackatee cheerfully, "except when Isham runs off at the head. He makes more enemies by shooting off his mouth than he can hire gunmen at ten dollars a day. That's me, you understand . . . I'm a hired *bravo,* as they call us in the Geronimo lingo, but when a man buys my services, he doesn't buy me, and I think what I dad-blamed please."

"Well, what do you think, then, of the Scarboroughs' methods of holding up strangers on the trail? I've seen some rough work, but the way they treated me made the blood fairly boil in my veins."

"It sure makes 'em sore," observed Meshackatee philosophically, "to be roped that way at the spring. And that hangman's knot and all, it's downright insulting . . . a man never quite gits over it."

"No, he doesn't," assented Hall, and rode on in brooding silence, for he was still in the hands of his enemies.

"And yet," went on Meshackatee, "it ain't what they do so much as the way they do it. You can take a man's gun without jabbing him in the belly and threatening to leave him for the buzzards, and, if you'd give 'em a few drinks and kinder jolly 'em along, the chances are that most of 'em would join. But that's the Scarboroughs, overbearing as hell, and nobody but a *Tejano* will stand for 'em. Jest the minute they saw your rigging, they was dead set ag'in' ye, because a Texican won't admit that a single-cinch saddle can be rode by a scholar and a gentleman. It's all double-rig with them, and tie to the horn, and any man that comes by with a dally-welter outfit is due to get a hazing. But I'm broadminded myself, and I sure throwed the hooks into 'em when I was telling about One-Eyed Tex. I was looking for Red to come through that stone door when I made that last crack about Texicans, and I still maintain that you can't hurt a *Tejano* by hitting him on the haid. I've heard 'em admit it themselves. And what I was telling you about them being from Uvalde is true as gospel script. They're the prize cow thieves in the world, bar none."

"Then how can you reconcile the matter with your conscience, if you accept money that has been gotten by stealing cows?"

Meshackatee grinned and scratched his shaggy beard, after a sudden, searching glance at his prisoner. "Well, in the first place," he said, "my conscience ain't the kind that worries much over trifles. And in the second place, this money never come from stealing cows . . . it's all in brand-new bills."

"New bills," repeated Hall, and then, after silence: "Well, where do they get these bills?"

"Search me." Meshackatee shrugged, still watching him narrowly. "Is that what you come to find out?"

"Why . . . why no!" exclaimed Hall. "Why certainly not. What gave you such a curious idea?"

"Ain't you an officer?" challenged Meshackatee. "I won't hold it ag'in' ye . . . might even be an officer myself! No? Honest? Gimme your word of honor? Well, somehow I can't hardly believe it. I go by hunches, see, and the first time I saw you, I says . . . 'There goes an officer!' But if you ain't, you ain't, and I know it's danged unhealthy for an officer that's caught in these parts. But it's the common report that this money of the Scarboroughs' was taken from a government paymaster."

"I see." Hall nodded, and his eyes flashed sudden fire although his face remained fixed like a mask.

"Yes," went on Meshackatee after waiting for him to speak, "and the government never forgets. Somebody robbed the ambulance and shot two or three soldiers, right up on the Camp Verde road, and you're the kind of man, if I was picking 'em out, that I'd send in to look the matter up."

"Nevertheless," returned Hall, "I must beg you to believe that I have nothing to do with such work. I'm a private citizen and the mission I'm on will not injure anyone in the world. I admit there was a time when I was drawn into a struggle that left a certain mark on my face, but that time is past, and someday, I trust, the marks will be less apparent. In brief, while I may have the look of a fighter, I come into this country with malice toward no man. I intend to remain strictly neutral."

"*Hmm,* neutral, eh?" Meshackatee sniffed, shifting his ponderous bulk and striking back the hair from one ear. "Do you see that little mark on my ear? Well, that broke me of being neutral."

Hall looked, and the lower lobe of the ear had been sliced down and left dangling by a segment—that's what the cowmen

26

call a jinglebob.

"I got that," went on Meshackatee, "in the Lincoln County War, when Billy the Kid was still working for Chisum and branding every cow brute he could rope. He'd ride along the road with a bunch of them tough cowboys, take the oxen out of them Mexican freight teams, and brand 'em while they was still in the yoke. That was Billy the Kid. But me, I was neutral. I wouldn't have no truck with such doings. Well, one night I was camping with another outsider when this outfit rode up . . . drunk.

" 'Who ye fur?' they says, and I speaks my little piece.

" 'I'm neutral,' I says, and they ropes me.

" 'A neutral's a maverick on this here range,' they says, and I'm a dog-goned Mexican if they didn't jinglebob my ears and burn a big fence rail on my ribs. Don't believe it, hey? Well, take a look at that and tell me if you're still a neutral!"

He tore open his shirt and exposed a long, red line, burned deeply into the tender flesh—then struck back the hair from his ears.

"That's the old Chisum brand"—he nodded grimly—"and they ran it on my pardner, too. He was a revengeful sort of cuss and tapped two of 'em, later. But me, I jest let my hair grow long and moved on to Arizona. But I've switched my system now, and whichever side is on the prod, I throw right in with them. It's the only way to do. Ain't it the innocent bystander that always gits shot in the neck? There's no principle involved . . . one's as bad as the other . . . so what's the use of being a fool? I'm out for the ready money. I'm a hired *bravo*, drawing my ten dollars a day and doing the heavy thinking for the gang, and, if you want to join in with us while you're looking for this party, I'll see that you get a job. Don't even have to stay with us if you don't like Isham's ways . . . go over and join the Bassetts and you'd be worth that much more than you

27

would be sticking around with the gang. But whatever you do, for cripes' sake don't stay neutral. You can see what happened to me."

He brushed back the hair over his slit and mangled ears and a steely look came into his eyes.

"I'm looking for a certain party myself," he said. "Reckon we all are . . . would you like to come in?"

"With you . . . yes," assented Hall, "but never with the Scarboroughs. I have taken a great dislike to Isham and his kind . . . and the ills that come to a man who stays neutral are nothing to what happens to a partisan. The partisan must fight whether he is right or wrong or be branded a traitor by his clan, and, if for one moment he shows kindness to an enemy, he is hounded by both sides alike. That is the unforgivable sin . . . any sign of humanity, any suggestion that the butchery should cease . . . and, as the fighting goes on, the worst element takes the lead while men of finer feeling drop out. And to drop out is to be branded a coward. But no man is truly brave until, for a principle, he is willing to be called a coward. And here, since you have shown me the rewards of being neutral, here is mine for being a partisan."

He stripped back his shirt—from the same left side that Meshackatee had bared to show his brand—and there, between two ribs, was a smooth round hole, where a bullet had passed through his body. It was a mere pit of red against the white skin, and just above the scar his heart beat on rhythmically as if nothing could still its pulse. Meshackatee stared, then leaned over closer and glanced up with a scared look in his eyes.

"How'd you happen to live?" he asked at last, and the stranger pointed solemnly to the sky.

"A miracle," he said, "if miracles still happen to men as unworthy as I am. I was left for dead . . . and so I still remain to those who sought my life . . . but I crawled to a cave and

28

recovered from my wound without medicine or care of any kind. In the mountains my name is added to the list of those who have died in the feud, but God has spared me . . . or so I think . . . to bring peace once more to Tug Fork."

"And where's that?" demanded Meshackatee, still staring at him curiously, and the stranger seemed to wake from a trance.

"I shouldn't have said that!" he burst out regretfully, "I shouldn't have mentioned Tug Fork. But as you are a gentleman. . . ." He paused expectantly and Meshackatee held out his hand. "Enough said," he told Hall, and they clasped hands in silence. For between gentlemen what need is there for words?

CHAPTER FOUR

The trail to Maverick Basin led north up Turkey Creek, and on both sides of the cañon, in caverns and beneath huge crags, the white houses of the cliff-dwellers caught the eye. The mountains rose up in jumbled and shattered terraces, split here and there by dark and jagged chasms that revealed the far heights beyond. These were covered with black pines and Douglas spruce, clinging close to the shelving slopes, and below them the oaks and junipers crept in, while at the bottom there was cactus and mesquite. It was a rough and thorny trail, winding in and out and up over brushy benches, then down again to the creek. Startled deer rose up timorously from their beds along the hillside; wild turkeys ran flapping across the path, and along the bluffs the tracks of mountain lion and bear told of others who prowled by night. But the scarcest track of all was that of man, the conqueror, who claims dominion over the birds and beasts. Like the lions and bears, men traveled by night or kept off the beaten trails.

Meshackatee rode ahead on a buckskin Indian pony that seemed to totter beneath his great weight, and, across the saddle in front of him, he balanced a repeating rifle with a bore like a buffalo gun. Behind followed Hall, still mounted on the blue roan that had so taken Red Scarborough's eye, and, scouting on before them, went Meshackatee's spotted dog, always seeking yet silent as a specter. The cañon opened out into wide, oak-clad flats with sycamores along the banks of the creek, and then the hills fell away to the east, giving a view of lone pinnacles beyond. They rode farther and the flats opened out into parks where deer and wild cattle grazed, and the high cliffs to the west came down nearer and nearer, as if to cut off their way. Then the trail left the creek and swung over toward the cliff and at Jump-Off Point it climbed the western rim and led north across Juniper Flats. They set off at a gallop, heading for a distant divide, and, as the sun was sinking low, they topped the last ridge and the basin lay smiling before them.

It was a wide and grassy valley, circled about with oak-crowned hills, and beyond it like a line the great Mogollon Rim stood out blue against the reddening sky. Tall pines, like half-stripped sticks, marked the edge of the unseen forest that covered the sloping plains beyond, and under the rim all the caved-off, lesser rims were smothered in a dense growth of trees. All else seemed shut in, overwhelmed, and obscured, but Maverick Basin lay set like a jewel within the curve of the golden-brown hills. It was a cowman's paradise, well watered with meandering streams and sheltered from north winds by the Mogollon Rim; its grass was all a-ripple; a wooded river bottom flanked the east, and live oaks made shade along its slopes. Yet here was where the Scarboroughs had settled down to make a little hell of their own.

Hall looked at it in silence, taking in its placid beauty and the roofs of peaceful houses among the trees, and, as he followed down the slope, he sighed.

"Gitting tired?" inquired Meshackatee. "Well, it ain't far now. See that long house, off to the west? That's the famous Rock House that the first settlers built to stand off the bloodthirsty Apaches, and now, by grab, it's got a bunch of Texas gunmen that could give 'em cards in spades. It's the Scarborough headquarters, and over to the east is the big log house of the Bassetts. It was built for Injuns, too . . . with loopholes and all . . . but it's too dog-goned close to that hill. The Rock House stands out in the middle of the plain, where you can't shoot it up from cover, but sure as hell, if they's ever any trouble, the Bassetts are going to git ambushed. They're right on the bank of Turkey Crick, too . . . where you see all them cottonwood trees . . . and a bunch of men could slip up through that brush and ketch 'em in the door at dawn. The other house, over north, it's the old Jensen place . . . they're using it now for a store.

"That's the first real house that was built in the basin," he went on with garrulous pride, "and it's sure seen doings in its day. Right there is where Jens Jensen made his start in the cow business and give the basin its name. Them first ones might have been mavericks, but the kind they're gitting now have been stole from as far as New Mexico. Jens was an honest old jasper, in a way . . . as honest as they let 'em git in these parts . . . but the bunch that come in later would rather steal a cow than have their breakfast in bed. They was so good with a running iron they could write their names with it, and everyone registered a brand that would burn spang over Jensen's. His iron was JJ and the Scarboroughs put pot-hooks on it that made it look like SS. The Bassetts jest altered the last J to JB connected and changed the first J to suit. Sharps Bassett worked it over into an S, like the Scarboroughs, and Winchester changed it to a W, and Bill, the black rascal, burned as pretty a WB connected as you've ever seen in your life. Oh, these boys git so good they take a pride in blotching brands and figuring out real elaborate burns . . . like that feller back in Texas that altered XIT into a five-pointed star and a cross. He was offered ten thousand dollars to show how he done it, and now they ain't a cotton picker this side of Uvalde that can't burn it over in his sleep. But that was back in Texas where the competition is strong. Out here, they was still in the ABC class, where a man used his initials for the brand. Well, they pulled off of Jens until they got halfway ashamed of themselves, he was such a peaceable old duck, and then Judge Malcolm comes driving into the basin with fifteen hundred head of cows. The judge had bought this stuff up in the San Juan country somewhere, or traded for it some way with them Mormons, and he come right in here, without by your leave or nothing, and turned them out on the range.

"All right, here was where the big doings began, because the Bassetts and the Scarboroughs claimed to control the whole basin and wouldn't let no settlers come in. That is, not unless they acknowledged their authority and gave 'em a hundred or so, but the judge . . . say, he was a freeborn American citizen and knowed it was public land. It was open to anybody and he turned his cows out on it, hiring a gunman or two to take charge, and the whole cussed outfit tied into him. The Scarboroughs and Bassetts was thick as thieves while they was running off the judge's cows, and the first thing he knowed he couldn't gather five hundred, and not a one of 'em under two years old. The picking was so good they heard about it back in Texas, and ever since that time, going onto two years now, these tough Texicans have been drifting in. Are they tough? They're so bad they'd have me scared if I hadn't seen Billy the Kid, but there was a killer that had 'em all beat . . . and he come from New York City. Never said nothing, either, always smiling and polite, and yet the dog-goned little shrimp had them bad Texans all buffaloed when he unlimbered and went to shooting.

"Oh, the judge? Well, he was a lawyer, all right. When he seen he couldn't stop 'em, and a couple of his gunmen got shot, he took the matter into court, but the whole basin rode down there, drunk and disorderly and loaded for bear, and swore out a warrant for him. That made the court judge sore, because the county was poor and he seen it was a neighborhood row, so he dismissed all the charges against everybody. This county is about as big as the state of Pennsylvania and mileage fees pile up quick, and the whole dog-goned outfit was nothing but a bunch of cow thieves, so what was the use of it, anyhow?

"Well, so far, so good, the wild bunch comes home and Judge Malcolm, he takes the big think. He's a lawyer, like I says, and them are the boys that know how to pull the right strings. He sends for the Scarboroughs and offers 'em a hundred head more, if they'll turn state's evidence and railroad the Bassetts. Well, the Bassetts are Injuns . . . and they'd made a little trouble when the Scarboroughs tried to run off some cows . . . so Isham and Red seen their chance to git shut of them and they took the hundred cows. They went down to Tonto and turned in their testimony, enough to send the Bassetts plumb to hell, but they talked so much they incriminated themselves and the judge threw the case out of court. But by now the Bassetts had got blood in their eyes and they come a-charging back, spent all their money on a lawyer, and had the Scarboroughs up for perjury. That sent Tonto County broke and court adjourned, but before they left town the judge or somebody gave the Maverick Basin crowd a quiet tip . . . the county was bankrupt, it was three days' hard riding for an officer to come up from Tonto, and the idee was they'd better keep out of court and settle their little differences with a Winchester."

"Oh, no," exclaimed Hall, "surely they didn't say that!"

"Mebbe not"—Meshackatee shrugged—"but they's one thing I know. There hasn't been an officer up here since."

Hall shook his head sadly and they rode on in silence, Meshackatee with his eyes on the Rock House far below them and Hall with his head bowed in thought. In his mind he was picturing the two contending factions and the battle that seemed certain to come, and, when he looked up, there was a strange light in his eyes and he gazed far away across the plain.

"But the other people," he suggested, "there are other settlers, too . . . could nothing be done with them?"

"What d'ye mean?" inquired Meshackatee, and Hall threw out his hands in a gesture of sudden appeal.

"Can't you see?" he cried. "This quarrel must be stopped before it has gone too far!"

"Oh, them," responded Meshackatee, tossing his head contemptuously, "they're afraid to call their souls their own. All that lives to the west, mostly, are friends of Isham's, and to the east and up Turkey Crick they're for the Bassetts, but they ain't ary one of 'em would stand up for his own rights, let alone throw a skeer into Isham. Because Isham is the man that's behind all this devilment . . . he's got ten hired gunmen, right now . . . and unless he's connected up with the United States mint he'll have to start something pretty soon."

"Yes, but what about the Bassetts? How can they expect to resist him unless they, too, hire more men?"

"They're broke," explained Meshackatee. "The lawyers got their money, and they ain't had the nerve to steal more. And then, being Injuns, they don't worry. They're three danged snaky *hombres*, to tell you the truth, and I don't want no trouble with none of 'em. Sharps is slow, but he's sure, and Winchester is quick and sure, and Bill, he's a fighting fool. He's whiter than the rest of 'em and he's jest naturally bad, proud of it, and don't care who knows it. That boy would fight a buzz saw with his hands tied behind him, if you'd listen to what he says. But ain't you heard the news? They've throwed in with Grimes, the big sheepman from up over the rim. He's a holy fighting terror that ain't afraid of nobody, or he wouldn't be up on that range. The Slashknife outfit has got cows there by the thousand, but that don't make no difference with Grimes. Every time he meets a cowboy or a bunch of these here rustlers, he drops down off his mule and commences to shoot, and . . . well, anyhow, he's promised to come down. He's going to bring his sheep and a bunch of fighting Mexicans and sheep out these bad *Tejanos*.

Well, you wait, and, if he comes, he'd better come a-shooting, because we got no use for sheep."

He shut his jaws down grimly and it was easy to see that he shared the cowman's prejudice against sheep.

"He ought to be kept out!" exclaimed Hall after a silence, and Meshackatee nodded approvingly.

"That's the talk," he praised. "I knowed you had it in you. Come on, and we'll turn the woollies back."

"No, I don't mean that," protested Hall. "What I mean is a man has no business to stir up trouble by deliberately invading a new range."

"Why sure," agreed Meshackatee heartily, "I'm with you, as big as a wolf. We'll jest go up that way tomorrow and talk reason to Mister Grimes, and maybe he'll decide not to come. No, I mean it, by grab . . . and, say, down at the house, I'll tell 'em you're jest a new man. They're rangy as the devil when they ketch some outsider . . . and, of course, you ain't a Texan . . . so I'll jest tell Miz Zoolah, that's Isham's wife, that you've come up to help with the sheep."

He spurred up his lagging mount and went galloping across the plain, but as they drew near the Rock House, he reined in suddenly, yet with his pony dancing nervously to go forward.

"Your name was Hall, wasn't it?" he inquired with a flourish. "All right, I'll fix it up. And, say, where you going, horse? What'd you say that other name was? You know, that feller you was looking for?"

"I didn't say," replied Hall, and, meeting his calm eyes, Meshackatee broke into a grin.

"Oh, that's right!" he exclaimed. "My mistake . . . excuse me!" And he jumped his dancing pony into a lope.

CHAPTER FIVE

The Rock House of the Scarboroughs was windowless and almost doorless, a long fort built of square-edged stone retrieved from an Indian ruin. In prehistoric days each stone had been quarried and carried on men's backs from the hills, but now their ancient city was a mound of tumbled rocks and its walls did new duty for the white man. The fort was built in frontier style, with narrow loopholes in place of windows and doorways just wide enough to pass—two rooms opening south and two opening north, with solid stone partitions between. Beneath the floor of the kitchen a well had been dug, to supply water in case of a siege, and the huge square chimney was loopholed near the top, making a watchtower to command the level plain.

In Indian days the old Rock House had served to protect the settlers from Apaches, but now the Scarboroughs, like robber barons of old, had turned it into a castle. Behind its thick walls they had grown prosperous and arrogant, and a big bunkhouse by the stable and corrals was swarming with feudal retainers. These were Texans to a man, and, as Hall rode up, they strolled over and eyed him coldly. That fatal single cinch on his California-rigged saddle had already aroused their antagonism, but their first fleering remarks were cut short by Miz Zoolah, who came bustling out of the kitchen. She was a dark, lanky woman with pale blue eyes that seemed to dart forth venom. After a single glance at Hall, she turned to Meshackatee who greeted her with deceptive meekness.

"Did you pass an Injun with a message for Isham?" she demanded in a threatening voice.

"No, ma'am," returned Meshackatee, "we didn't pass nobody. What's the news . . . have the sheep come in?"

"Yes, the sheep have come in," she burst out angrily, "and Elmo and these trifling cowboys have let 'em. They just watched the main trail and Grimes made another one and came in across the reservation. He's halfway down Cañon Creek now!"

"Well?" inquired Meshackatee, rolling his eyes at the Texans, and Miz Zoolah flew into a tantrum.

"They're afraid!" she cried. "Elmo and all the rest of 'em! They're afraid to go out and move him. But just wait till Isham comes back and I'll bet there'll be a scattering of sheep."

"Very likely," observed Meshackatee. "This is Mister Hall, Missus Scarborough. He's a new man we picked up down below."

"Well, if he don't turn out any better than some that we've got, you might as well tell him to go. I declare, when this Grimes and his Mexicans began shooting, Elmo and all of them gave him the trail."

"Shooting?" repeated Meshackatee, arching his eyebrows inquiringly, and Mrs. Scarborough nodded her head.

"Yes, shooting," she said. "The minute he saw them, he dropped down and emptied his Winchester. And him a dirty sheepman, with nothing but Mexicans, and these boys all claim they're from Texas. I'd just like to know what we've been paying them for if it isn't to stand up and fight, but they turned tail and ran and I'm going to tell Isham that he ought to fire them all!"

"Oh, I don't know," murmured Meshackatee, glancing at the shamefaced cowboys, "you'd jest have to hire some more. What's the chances for something to eat?"

"You can eat with the rest of them," she answered impatiently, "and not a minute before. Now you worthless cowboys go away from that kitchen and quit making eyes at the cook. And if you want to hurry supper, somebody take the axe and chop up a little wood."

There was a rush for the axe and the cowboys slouched away, laughing hectoringly at the man who had won.

"Well, git down," said Mrs. Scarborough with a grudging sigh, "that makes fourteen men we're cooking for."

They dismounted stiffly and she drew Meshackatee aside, talking rapidly as he inclined his curly head, and then, as Hall stood awkwardly by, a girl hurried out the kitchen door. In one hand was a huge bucket and she had started for the well when she met the newcomer's startled eyes. For a moment she stood still, then the bucket fell with a *clatter* and was clutched up with a trembling hand.

"Let me help you," said Hall, raising his hat and advancing swiftly.

While Meshackatee looked on, he filled the bucket with practiced hand and carried it back to the kitchen. There was a murmur of disapproval from the gunmen by the bunkhouse as he did not emerge immediately, and Mrs. Scarborough glanced around suspiciously, but he returned to his horse without meeting her eyes and Meshackatee grinned to himself.

The kitchen was forbidden ground at the ranch, hence the rush to chop and bring in the wood, but this stranger had shown himself adept indeed at invading the *sanctum sanctorum*. He had met Mrs. Scarborough's niece and filled her bucket and whisked it back into the house, in about the time it would take a Texan to spit out his chew of tobacco. But that dropping of the bucket—was Miss Allifair so flustered, or had it been done with a purpose? He listened gravely to Miz Zoolah as she asked him questions and then guessed at the answers herself, but all the while his keen eyes were on Hall and his mind was seeking out the cause. For there is a reason for everything, if one can piece facts together or even jump at the facts, and Meshackatee was by nature a casuist. But something of the furor that was going on in his mind seemed to be communicated to the vigilant Miz Zoolah, for she stopped in the middle of a spiteful tirade and turned her pale eyes on the stranger.

"Who is that man?" she demanded suddenly, and then she advanced and faced him. "Haven't I seen you before somewhere?" she questioned sharply.

Hall seemed to rouse from some dream. "No, ma'am," he replied in soft, reassuring tones, "or at least, ma'am, not to my knowledge. I am a stranger in these parts and. . . ."

"Where'd you come from?" she put in, and he hesitated a moment before he made an answer.

"I am sorry," he said, "but I can't answer that question. I am just passing through and. . . ."

"Who is this man?" she demanded of Meshackatee, and, as she repeated the question, a swift look passed between them and the two men joined forces against her.

"I don't know," returned Meshackatee, "but he's a stranger in this country . . . the boys picked him up at Cold Spring. Isham told me to bring him up here, but there's nothing against him. It was jest to protect him from the Bassetts."

"Yes, the Bassetts," she snapped. "He must be a weakling if he needs any protection from them."

"Well, he's my prisoner, then," spoke up Meshackatee bluffly. "Anything else you'd like to know?"

"Yes, I'd just like to know why you allowed him in that kitchen if Isham sent him over as a prisoner. He might have stepped out that farther door and been halfway over to the Bassetts."

"He gave me his word of honor," answered Meshackatee defiantly. "I guess there's such a thing as a gentleman."

"A gentleman!" she shrilled. "He gave you his word of honor! Since when have you got these ideas into your head? I'm going to report this to Isham."

"Well, report and be blowed!" burst out Meshackatee rudely, and led his prisoner away.

But even in a world where honor is not dead and the word "gentleman" is more than a name, there is such a thing as a reasonable precaution and Meshackatee slept by his man that night. They threw down their saddle blankets beneath the towering cottonwood that stood just north of the house, and he slept with his dog at his back. It was the way they always slept, back to back on the scant blanket, and, if anything moved, 'Pache would raise his head and give voice to a rumbling growl.

The night was well along when there was a stir at his back and the vibrations of a noiseless growl. Meshackatee opened his eyes and moved gently in answer and a strange sight met his eyes. His prisoner had risen up without a sound and tiptoed back toward the house, and, as he stood in the starlight, a white form glided out and met him in passionate embrace. Meshackatee moved again and his dog sank down obediently—there was a silence, and the prisoner came back—but far into the night the man who was a casuist lay and speculated on the ultimate cause.

CHAPTER SIX

It is easy to find a probable cause for any given act, but when one seeks the ultimate cause—the reason behind it all—that calls for deep thinking, and finesse. Human conduct is not so variable in many of its phases as to call for extended scrutiny, but the problem before Meshackatee was both so baffling and so disquieting that it left his brain in a whirl. That a girl as modest as Allifair Randolph, a woman who for months had received the attentions of scores of cowboys without one answering smile, should suddenly and for no reason throw aside all decorum and rush into the arms of a stranger—that was beyond the bounds of reason. It was so unreasonable it was foolish, and the great cause must be sought somewhere else. Surely they had met before. Yes, met and learned to love, and this was the reunion of two souls that had drifted far apart. Allifair was that certain party for whom Hall had been seeking, and he had found her in the kitchen of the Scarboroughs.

Yet this comforting conclusion, plain and obvious as it was, merely opened up new fields of thought. Who was Allifair Randolph and who was this man Hall, and why did they conceal their love, and what would he do now, since he had discovered his beloved in the house of the man he despised? Would he cast aside his scruples against feuds and cattle wars and join the gang to be near her, or would he go his way and devise other means of winning the woman of his heart? Meshackatee thought it over, and then his scheming mind began to turn the facts to his own purpose. When the morning came, he beckoned to his prisoner and led him across the creek to the mound. Here, beneath a gnarled oak that had grown up near the summit, drawing its strength from the dust of ancient dead, Meshackatee took out his field glasses and gazed long to the east before he broached the matter on his mind.

To the east lay Turkey Creek and the log fort of the Bassetts—and Grimes and his Mexicans as well—and it was to them fully as much as to the winning over of this stranger that his thoughts were turned that day. He had a dual mind, one part taking cognizance of the facts and the other busily using them to work his will. When he spoke, it was all to fit his program, although disguised in the mock solemnity of a jest.

"Mister Hall," he began, "I make it a principle never to interfere in the private affairs of any gentleman, but I saw something last night which pained me very much and I jest want to ask a few questions. Now in the first place, Mister Hall, I want you to understand that Miss Allifair holds a high place in my regard, and I jest want to ask . . . as a friend, you understand . . . if your intentions are perfectly honorable?"

"My intentions?" faltered Hall, and then he went white and turned his face away. "Don't tell anybody," he pleaded, "it would ruin our happiness forever. Oh, I was mad . . . insane . . . I should never have done it. But Meshackatee . . . she had thought I was dead."

"Oh, dead, eh?" rumbled Meshackatee, squinting his calculating eyes and regarding him from beneath his long hair. "Well, that makes a difference, of course. She'd heard about that shooting, and the bullet hole under your heart, and. . . ."

"That's it . . . they told her I was dead," Hall said, turning again toward Meshackatee.

"They?"

"Yes. Her folks, and Missus Scarborough. She was a Randolph, you know, before her marriage, and she told Allifair I was dead."

"I see," observed Meshackatee, nodding his head and spitting wisely, "and was you young folks engaged to git married?"

"That was it, that's what caused it. We were engaged to be married, but we belonged to opposing clans. She was a Randolph, you see, and I'm a McIvor. . . ."

"Ah," exclaimed Meshackatee, "I'm beginning to savvy! The Randolph-McIvor feud, back in Kaintuck."

"Yes, that's it," went on Hall feverishly, "but let me explain it to you. Our families have been at war for over twenty years, and each year the feud becomes worse. It's cost the Randolph faction over four hundred dead and the McIvors over three hundred that we know of. Men are found dead in the woods, just as I was left for dead, and others are never found. All our relatives are engaged in it, and hundreds of outsiders who hardly know what they're fighting for. All they think of is free whiskey and midnight raids and a chance to get revenge on some enemy, and so it goes until the mountains are a battleground and men have turned to brutes. And there's no power that can stop it, neither the courts nor the militia, because we live far back in the hills. But if I could marry Allifair, then the blood feud would be ended and the Randolphs and McIvors would be friends."

"I understand," murmured Meshackatee, and sat smiling benevolently as the young man gazed off into space.

"We met by accident," he went on at last, "while I was scouting in their country. But she spared my life, she did not report me, and the next time we met we were friends. She's such a gentle creature . . . and I had turned rough, from living and fighting for years, but somehow she learned to love me and the dream came to both of us to marry and end the feud. I was building a cabin, far up in the hills where no one would ever find us, when a dirty little spy discovered our meeting place and the Randolphs became aware of our plans. They watched us . . . and the next time I went to our tree, there was no one there, she was gone. They reported her dead . . . shot down by the McIvors, for our womenfolk make war among themselves . . . but I asked all our women and none of them had done it, though many of them would gladly have done so.

"Can you imagine such conditions . . . gentle women, well educated, going out like wild animals to strike down a woman like Allifair? I must have gone mad, for I went back to our meeting place, and there this dirty spy shot me. He shot me clean through the heart, or so it appeared, but the bullet went low, and, after they had left me, I came to life and crept to a cave. There I lived on pure water for eleven days, and, as my body became purified, I had visions and dreams, such as no man ever had before. And when I was well, I crept up by night and listened at a camp of the Randolphs. That was where I heard that Allifair still lived and had been sent out to her aunt in Arizona. But what her aunt's name was, or where her husband lived, was something I never could learn, so I left and came out here, determined to find her if it took the rest of my life."

"Well, you've found her," observed Meshackatee, apparently unruffled by the harrowing tale of his friend, "so what's the next thing now?"

"They'll kill her!" he groaned, "they'll actually kill her before they'll consent to her marrying a McIvor. So, if you want to kill me, too, and ruin both our lives, just tell who I am to the Scarboroughs."

"Oh, no, oh, no," replied Meshackatee reassuringly, "that won't be necessary at all. Of course I'm working for Isham, and, when I take a man's money, I aim to give him my best, but it won't be necessary . . . that is, always provided you're willing to help me out?"

"I'll do anything," promised Hall, "if you'll just keep our secret and help me to meet her again. Oh, since I have seen her and learned she still loves me, I feel I could do anything . . . anything."

"*Hmm,* a meeting ain't so easy," said Meshackatee after a silence. "Miz Zoolah sure keeps a close watch. But you leave it to me, boy, and meanwhile stay away from her. I ain't the only man that has eyes. Them Texas toughs are jealous . . . they seen you go in there yesterday . . . so keep plumb out of that kitchen. And the look in that gal's eyes when she seen you at the well gave the whole business away, to me. You're kind of daffy now, don't notice where you're going or answer when other people speak to you, so the best thing for you is to go away for a few days and let this excitement die down. Now I've got a little job, if you think you can do it."

"Oh, I can't leave her now," protested Hall broken-heartedly, but Meshackatee tapped him sharply on the shoulder.

"You're going to leave, see? Right now and no danged fooling. You're going over to hunt up them sheep."

"The sheep?" repeated Hall, and Meshackatee smiled grimly as he took him gently by the arm.

"Take my advice," he warned, "and git away from Miz Zoolah . . . she came almighty close to recognizing you. Now about this sheepman, Grimes, he knows these boys by sight and they can't any of 'em git near him, but that saddle of yours will tell anyone you're no Texan, and I believe you can ride plumb up to him. You're a stranger, see, and you can cuss out the Scarboroughs and tell him all the things they done to you, and, after you've got next to him and found out all his plans, you come back here and tell me. Do that, and you'll git to see Allifair."

"Well, it's treacherous," observed Hall at last, "but I've been that, and worse, before now. And if this man is coming in to stir up a war, perhaps I can turn him back."

"This is what will turn him back," returned Meshackatee, patting his pistol, "and, believe me, nothing else. That *hombre* is a fighter. He comes on a-charging, and nothing but a bullet will stop him. But leave that to me and this bunch of inbred Texans . . . and by the way, that's Isham coming."

He pointed to the cañon down which they had come and two horsemen, riding fast, flashed around a point and came galloping across the plain.

"You'd better wait," suggested Meshackatee, "you're supposed to be a prisoner, and maybe he'll have other plans."

"I'm not working for him," declared Hall obstinately. "I'm doing this work for you."

"Fair enough," agreed Meshackatee, "but I'm working for him. So try to stand in on the play. Come on, we'll go down to the house."

They arrived just as Elmo, the youngest of the Scarboroughs, stepped out from where he had been skulking. He was short and sandy, with a slouchy wool hat and two guns hung low on his hips. Each was tied at the bottom with a buckskin string that held the muzzles close to his legs, so that the carved ivory handles stuck out at such an angle that they practically touched his hands. Both holsters were cut away until they barely held their pistols, and the whole was arranged so that he could draw and shoot in the shortest possible time. But the boy himself— for he was hardly a man—had on his face such a look of both weakness and reckless deviltry that Hall looked him over again. He was sullen now, after his defeat by the sheepmen and the tongue-lashing that Miz Zoolah had given him, but he stepped out to meet his brothers with such a purposeful swagger that Mrs. Scarborough allowed him to pass.

"Well, they've come, boys," he announced, "Dave Grimes and twenty Mexicans, and nigh onto ten thousand sheep. They got in behind us, come across the reservation, and now they're headed for the basin."

"Let 'em come!" challenged Isham, dropping down off his horse, "that suits me to a hickey . . . let 'em come. But the first damned Mexican that puts a sheep across Turkey Crick is going to git killed, that's all. That's my deadline . . . Turkey Crick . . . and the minute they step across it the fireworks is going to begin."

"We thought we'd better wait," explained Elmo hastily, "until you and Red got home. . . ."

"That's right, kid," praised Isham, "you've got the right idée . . . leave it to me, and they won't nobody git hurt. But if you go riding in on 'em when they're down on their knees and shooting. . . ."

Elmo glanced at Miz Zoolah and spit a thin jet of tobacco juice, while the Texas gunmen smirked. But Miz Zoolah was not the woman to let this pass unchallenged and she stepped out and confronted her husband.

"Do you happen to know," she demanded contentiously, "that Elmo and these cowboys ran away? Well, they did . . . ran away from those Mexicans like cowards . . . and now look at the way they act."

The cowboys winced but Isham was excited and he paid scant attention to his helpmeet.

"Now come on, boys," he ordered, "ketch up your horses and git ready and we'll go out and meet the damned Mexicans. But no shooting, savvy, until I give the word, unless they shoot at us first."

He paced up and down while they ran to saddle their horses and Miz Zoolah assailed his ears with complaints, but he only glanced at her absently, slapping his boot with his quirt and staring off toward the Bassetts'.

"Where are them sorry blacks at?" he demanded of Me-shackatee. "Have you seen 'em around this morning? The dirty, half-Injun bastards, they may be laying in wait for us . . . better send somebody over to the store."

"I'll go!" volunteered Elmo, making a run to mount his horse, but Isham motioned him back.

"You look out, kid," he warned, "them Injuns are treacherous. They're liable to shoot you from the brush."

He turned to Meshackatee, and, as they consulted together, Hall felt Isham's eyes fixed upon him. Beneath their bleached, white lashes they regarded him coldly, as if appraising his worth as a spy, and at last, as Meshackatee drove his point home and nailed it, the chief of the Scarboroughs beckoned. But Hall stood firm, his mouth grimly set, his eyes far away on the hills, and Meshackatee understood.

"I'll tell him," he said, and half an hour later Hall rode forth over toward the store.

CHAPTER SEVEN

The trail to the store led across the level valley, tramped broad by the passing of many horse herds, and, as Hall left the Rock House and rode out into the open, more than one watchful eye was upon him. Yet he jogged on at a foxtrot, never turning to look back at the gathering clan of the Scarboroughs, and, as he neared the store, a single horseman left the Bassetts and rode warily over to meet him. It was the first move in the great conflict that was sure to take place when the Scarboroughs and Bassetts, after years of petty bickerings, would meet and fight it out. Time and again they had swooped down and challenged each other, only to withdraw with loud boasts and threats, but now that the sheep had invaded the basin, it was war, and war to the knife. For as cattle and sheep cannot live together, but one or the other is sure to take the range, so the Bassetts and the Scarboroughs could not live in Maverick Basin—and the first blow would start a bloody feud.

All this Hall sensed, for years of mountain warfare had made him quick to read the minds of lawless men. But their battles were not his, and, as he approached the shabby store, he dismounted and left his rifle on his horse. The store was a log cabin, set off to one side from the foundations of a house that had been burned, and within its loopholed walls there was everything for sale, from horseshoes to cornmeal and whiskey. The storekeeper came out, smiling and wringing his hands—a cringing little man with mouse-colored hair and a nervous, insinuating smile—but, as he wrapped up his few purchases, Hall did not fail to notice that his eyes never left the door. There was a thud of hoofs without, a long, tense silence, and then a shadow fell across the doorway.

He came in sideways, a thick-set, swarthy man with a sparse black beard and mustache, and, as Hall looked up, he met a pair of glittering eyes that searched him through and through.

"Good morning," he said, but the man did not answer and Hall went on with his buying.

"Oh, *er* . . . Sharps," stammered the storekeeper, whose name was Johnson, "this is Mister . . . *er* . . . ?"

"Hall," replied the stranger without looking up, but the storekeeper was not to be discouraged. With all his fawning ways he had a name as a busybody and now he was starting to live up to it.

"Oh, yes . . . Hall." He cringed. "You're new in the basin. Are you staying over at the Scarboroughs?"

"No," returned Hall, and the Indian eyes of Sharps Bassett seemed to stab him in the back for a liar. "I'm just riding through," he explained at length, and instantly the storekeeper asked where. Then, without waiting for the answer, he darted to the doorway, and Bassett stepped out behind him. Hall followed them quickly, for they were gazing to the south, and, as he looked down the trail, he saw the gunmen from the Rock House riding in with the Scarboroughs at their head. They came on at a gallop, letting out shrill yips and yelps and rollicking about in their saddles. As they thundered up to the store, Sharps reached for his rifle and put his broad back to the wall.

"Oh, here you are," sneered Isham as Sharps faced him stolidly. "Well, you sorry, black bastard, I want to warn ye for the last time not to bring them sheep into this basin. This is a white man's country and you've got no business here nohow, but if you bring in them Mexicans, we'll run them out first, and

51

then we'll run you out. What d'ye think you was going to do . . . shoot this man in the back while he was buying a plug of tobaccy? Well, we've got you, Mister Injun, this trip."

Sharps grunted contemptuously and shifted his eyes, and, as the Texans followed his glance, they saw two other horsemen, riding rapidly in from the east. They came on at a gallop, then reined in their fine horses and trotted gracefully up to the store. It was Winchester Bassett and Bill.

Bill was nothing but a boy, lighter complected than his brothers but with the same heavy, half-Indian face, and, as he rode up beside Sharps, he stuck out his chin and made a mouth at the swaggering Elmo.

"Hello there, Squirley!" he hailed insultingly, and Winchester told him to shut up. Winchester Bassett was tall and slenderly built, with a heavy black mustache and a lightning-like quickness of eye, but, as he reproved his younger brother, he had a smile of easy tolerance, and young Bill was by no means abashed. They both dropped to the ground, and, as they lined up beside Sharps, the Texans reined their horses away. It was a challenge, a defiance to the whole Scarborough clan that had ridden up and surrounded their chief. As the Scarboroughs gave back, Winchester smiled again, for he saw that their bluff had been called. They had galloped over to the store to catch Sharps by himself and worry him as dogs do a wolf, but Sharps had stood them off and now the other two had joined him— three men against fifteen, but determined. And three men on foot, with the firm ground to shoot from, might easily come off the victors, for the horses of the Texans, being wild and half-broken, would jump at the very first shot.

But no shot would be fired—or not at that time—for Isham had given the word to stand back, and, as the gunmen grinned and weakened, even Sharps's snake-like eyes took on a glint that was Indian for a smile. He was all Indian, this eldest of the fighting Bassett tribe, slow and stolid but immovable as a wall. No matter what the odds, Sharps Bassett would never run, and his old battered rifle had killed more bears and lions than any other gun in the country. He stood there now like a grizzly bear at bay, and Bill, seeing the Texans filing in for a drink, turned his eyes to the smart-aleck Elmo.

"Put down that gun," he challenged as Elmo began to roll his pistol, "and I'll come over there and whip you."

"I don't haf to!" retorted Elmo, raising his pistol with a flourish and riding out past a tree, and, as he whirled his horse, he put six shots into the tree trunk, coming by it on the gallop.

"Beat that," he said, "and I'll show you some real shooting. I can put up a six-spot and shoot out every pip with my horse going by on the run."

"Don't you worry," bantered Bill, "I kin shoot straight enough, as you'll find out, if it comes to a showdown. I thought you was going to do something."

He laughed as a Texan told him gruffly to hush up, and then he returned to Elmo.

"Put up that danged smoke-house," he called out hectoringly, "you ain't got the guts to use it. Jest meet me halfway and I'll fight you, fist and skull . . . for the drinks or for nothing at all."

He laid off his belt with the two six-shooters hung loosely in it, and stepped out into the open, but Elmo declined to fight. Some of the gunmen urged him on, but he had fought Bill once before and come off second best.

"Aw, come away, Bill," jeered Winchester, "can't you see he's afraid to fight ye? Come on, let's go back home."

"Well, you're so danged fresh," flared up Isham, stepping forward, "you come, and I'll fight you myself."

"Nope, don't want no trouble," answered Winchester quietly. "Git your horse, Bill, we'll be going home."

"You're skeered!" taunted Isham, laying off his belted pistols and rolling up his sleeves defiantly, but Winchester only smiled.

"You might gang me," he said, but, as Isham began to whoop, Sharps Bassett suddenly laid off his belt. Shaking the black hair from his eyes, he advanced without a word, his neck swelling like a blow snake's with rage.

"I'll fight ye," he rumbled, and Isham backed away, then turned and made a jump for his guns.

"You dirty, black scoundrel!" he yelled in a false fury, "don't you think I seen that knife in your boot? I wouldn't dirty my hands on a nigger like you, nohow . . . because that's all you are, a damned nigger!"

Sharps stood in the open, his huge fists still clenched, his eyes turning red with savage rage, then he, too, wheeled and reached for his guns. There was a silence, and the gunmen that Isham had hired crouched low and waited for the break, but, before a hand had moved, a man stepped swiftly forward and took his place beside the Bassetts. It was Hall McIvor, and, as the Texans paused to glance at him, the tenseness of the moment was broken. A new emotion stepped in, to break the psychic wave that was sweeping them on toward a killing.

"What are you doing . . . over there?" demanded Isham roughly, and Hall fixed him with his piercing black eyes.

"I'm here to fight," he answered quietly. "This is no quarrel of mine, but when fifteen men pitch on three, I'm going to help them, right or wrong."

"You half-Injun rascal!" burst out Isham accusingly. "I said all the time you was here to join the Bassetts . . . and now, by Godfrey, look at him!"

He turned to Meshackatee, who was looking on in wonder, and pointed a scornful hand at their ex-prisoner, but Hall's blood was up, and, as Isham continued to point, he leaped over and slapped him in the face.

"Take that," he said, "and, if you pretend to be a gentleman, draw your gun and we'll shoot this out!"

He stood expectantly, his slim hand poised and waiting above the butt of a well-worn pistol, but Scarborough did not go for his gun. He hesitated, and, as Hall saw the fear in his eyes, he stepped back with a thin-lipped smile.

"In my country," he said, "we settle our differences of opinion by stepping off ten paces, then turn and shoot. I say you are a coward, a blustering fool, and no gentleman . . . do you accept my challenge, or not?"

"Aw, you're crazy," muttered Isham, backing off into the crowd, and Hall let it pass. But when the Scarboroughs were gone, he glanced swiftly at Winchester Bassett, who responded with his unruffled smile.

CHAPTER EIGHT

Nothing had been further from the intentions of Hall McIvor as he rode forth from the Rock House that morning than that he should join the Bassetts as a friend. He had been sent to join them, yes, but treacherously, as a spy, who was to return and report to Meshackatee. But his heart had ruled his head—he had joined against the Scarboroughs and then slapped Isham in the face—and now that it was over he found himself a turncoat, shaking hands with Winchester Bassett. Yet something still told him that his heart had been right, and that open friendship was better than treachery, and that somehow, somewhere, he would see Allifair again, although never under the protection of the Scarboroughs.

Yet protection he must have, if he was to remain near her at all, and he sought it under the roof of the Bassetts. They lived in a log house set on the edge of the river bottom, but with its single, narrow door facing away from the creekbed and out upon the level plain. Its timbers were squarely hewn, with loopholes in place of windows, and the fireplace at one end was as massive as the Scarboroughs', with holes near the top for a look-out. A barn and round corral, for breaking horses, stood farther along on the bench and, beyond and to the south, rose the high, wooded hill that Meshackatee had predicted would be an ambush. A pack of hounds rushed out to greet them, hogs and chickens strayed about the yard, and, as Hall rode up to the gate, an old white-haired man hobbled out.

"Eh . . . what was the name?" he quavered anxiously, staring up at him with his far-sighted eyes. "Oh, Hall, eh? Well, git down, git down, Mister Hall. We ain't got much, but what we have, you're shorely welcome to . . . our latch string is always hung out. What's the news, boys?" he demanded. "Did you rout them biggoty Scarboroughs? Well, good, and good again. Them and their no-account Texas gunmen . . . one Bassett could whip a hundred of 'em."

"Well, we whipped 'em, Pap," returned Winchester, "and this gentleman here slapped Isham's face and called him a dirty coward."

"He did," exulted old Henry, turning to take Hall by the arm, "well now, don't that beat all. And him a stranger, too . . . but he looks like a fighting man! What did Isham say to that?"

"He didn't say nothing." Winchester laughed. "Jest mounted his *caballo* and flew."

Henry Bassett stopped short to join in with silent laughter, and then he led the way to the house. He was shriveled and bent, with a long, white beard and hands that clutched and clawed it when he talked, but his high, hawk-like nose and resolute eyes told of a courage that never had waned. Of all his boys, the swarthy Winchester was most like him, while Bill was whiter by far. But Bill had the heavy jaw and fat-cheeked face that came from his Digger Indian mother, and Sharps would pass for a full-blood anywhere, except for his chilled-steel nerve. Not a word had he said since his challenge to Isham, and his beady black eyes still glinted with anger as he slouched along out to the corrals. His rage, or so it seemed, now included the whole white race, and he stared at Hall evilly.

The interior of the Bassett fort was dark and smoky, and, as they moved over toward the fireplace, an Indian woman rose up and padded silently away. She was old Henry's wife, or "woman" as he called her, but none of the men spoke to her, and, when she came back, her presence was studiously ignored.

"Have a cheer! Have a cheer!" urged Henry cordially, motioning Hall to a seat by the fire. "So you and my cubs whipped Isham again! Well, well, I'd 'a' liked to ben there. But my eyes ain't what they was and my legs is bothering some, so I aim to hold the fort here at home. I went out last week, when my hounds bayed a lion, and it kinder fetched my rheumatiz back. But them no-account Scarboroughs, I'd fight ary one of 'em with any weepon he'd name . . . from the p'int of a needle to the muzzle of a shotgun. I shore do despise that Isham!"

"He offered to fight Winchester!" spoke up Bill with a grin, "but Winch said he didn't want no trouble. And then, when Isham begin to crow, Sharps stepped out and offered to whip him. Hand and skull, it was, but Isham was afraid of him, so he backed off and went to calling names. I'd've plugged him right there, but Winch wouldn't let me, and, while we was waiting for 'em to make a crooked move, this feller here comes over and joined us. He says the Scarboroughs held him up down in Deadman Cañon and threatened to hang him for a horse thief, and he don't allow no man to treat him like that, so he challenged old Isham to a duel."

"He did," shrilled old Henry. "Well, what did Isham do?"

"He jest said . . . 'You're crazy,' . . . and backed away outer that, before all four of us blowed him full of holes."

"Well, well"—Henry beamed—"you must be a Southerner, I reckon, to be talking of fighting a duel. It ain't done much out here. They run more to bushwhacking and shooting a man in his door, but back in Tennessee, where I was born and raised, they had duels every court day. I've seen two mountain men grab the ends of a handkerchief and cut and slash away with their Bowie knives till one or the other dropped dead, but these Texans are so treacherous they'd shore shoot you in the back before you'd stepped off five paces. A duel is for gentlemen, but

I don't count them Scarboroughs as human . . . and I told 'em so pointedly one time. They've abused me and my boys till we won't stand it no more, and someday they's going to be a killing. I'm a peaceable man, but I can't git no jestice . . . leastwise I can't git it in the courts . . . and, when they went to hiring gunmen, they forced my hand and I had to throw in with them sheepmen. Don't like sheep, I reckon, any more than you do, but Grimes and his Mexicans are fighters. They'll shore put a torch under them Texas bad men that'll burn 'em off the face of the earth. Me and my cubs ain't robbed no bank, nor paymaster's wagon neither, and we ain't got the money to hire gunmen, but after Grimes has got through with 'em, I reckon the Bassetts can clean up on what there is left."

He winked and nodded wisely, and, as the boys sat down, the squaw after a silence came timidly in and went on with cooking the dinner. She was still strong and vigorous, although her hair was turning gray, and from time to time, as old Henry ran on, she glanced up at him with grave, adoring eyes.

"Yes, they call me a squawman," he confessed confidentially, when his wife had left them alone again, "but I've had other women and they was never a one of 'em that suited me as well as this one. I thought I'd git rid of her when I come to this country, taking Sharps and Winchester with me, but she located me somehow and come a thousand miles overland, bringing Bill along on her back. That's faithfulness, I say, and I let her stay with me . . . and she shore thinks the world of old Hank."

He smiled complacently as she came back to her kitchen, the hearth and hobs of the fireplace, and squatted down to look into the Dutch ovens, and, when she was gone once more, he jerked his head knowingly and lowered his voice again.

"Don't you worry," he said, "she savvies what's going on . . . understands every word I say, but you can't git her to speak English, not unless the house ketches afire or a horse gits down in the barn. She's afraid of them Scarboroughs. She claims they're bad medicine . . . 'All same snake in the grass.' . . . but this sheepman, Grimes, will shore crush their head, though their head may bruise his heel. That's what the Scripture says, according to Grimes . . . he's religious, some kind of a jack Mormon. Calls 'em brother when he's among 'em and sons of dogs when he's away from 'em, the same as all these other danged sheepmen. I never did like a sheep, to tell you the truth, but what else is they to do? If I don't bring in Grimes, them Scarboroughs are fixing to git me, and run me and my boys out of the country. Ain't a man got a right to protect his home? They crowded me to it, that's all."

The old man spent the day denouncing the meanness of the Scarboroughs and justifying his alliance with Grimes, but when, in the evening, Grimes himself rode in, Hall could see he was none too welcome. He was cordially received, for that was their custom, but after the first greetings the talk died down to nothing and the sheepman cast about for a listener. He was a big, burly man with a Scotch turn to his tongue, and, when he talked, he thrust out his head vehemently and showed the bloodshot whites of his eyes. A month's growth of beard did not add to his appearance, and the hair lay in a mat on his chest, and he seemed to be mad, mad all the time, with a primal caveman's rage.

"I'll show 'em, the dirty cowards!" he burst out vindictively, addressing his harangue to Hall McIvor. "Did you ever see a cowman that would stand up to a Winchester? Well, I haven't, and yet I've seen lots of them. That Slashknife outfit now is reputed to be a bad one, and they lay claim to the whole upper range, but here's one sheepman that they've never moved yet, and, what's more, they never will. I can ride across there any place and they'll give me the trail. They know me as far as they can see me through a telescope. And these herders of mine, though they're nothing but Mexicans, are proper fighting fools . . . every one. I won't have 'em otherwise, and the first man that weakens, I make him walk back to town. We're coming here tomorrow with ten thousand sheep under a lease from Henry Bassett. That gives us a right, don't it? We're running them on shares, and this has always been his range. But if any of them smart gunmen, like they tried to do yesterday, ride in and interfere with my herders, I ain't saying nothing, I'll jest drop off my mule, and shoot the matter out, right there."

"That's your privilege," conceded Hall, "but wouldn't it be better to stay on the east side of Turkey Creek?"

"One side or the other . . . it's nothing to me. This is government land, see? And I'm a U.S. citizen. These deadlines don't go with me."

Hall nodded and fell silent, for he knew the Scotch blood, but Grimes was pacing the floor.

"They'll draw a deadline, will they?" he demanded menacingly. "They'll tell me where I'll go and not go? I'm a free agent, see? I know what's my rights, and I don't give a damn for the Scarboroughs. Didn't I meet their men yesterday, up on the Cañon Crick trail? Yes, and the whole suffering outfit rode over the top of a mountain to git away from my gun. You couldn't see 'em for dust, they were that anxious to escape me . . . if they'd had a feather in their hand, they'd've flew . . . and now they send word that they've made a new deadline, only this time it's Turkey Crick. I'll show 'em a deadline, and I'll go out and kill a cow every time they kill one of my sheep. They's no law here and I know it, so we'll get back to first principles and fight it out man to man. If you ever read any poetry, you may remember those famous lines about Rob Roy and the good, old simple plan . . . 'That they should take who have the power and they should keep who can.' That was the plan back in Scotland for many a long year, and it's the plan out here today, and I, for one, will never speak against it, for it has served me well so far."

"Apparently so," replied Hall, who was beginning to turn against him. "I suppose every man follows his own nature."

"What do you mean, my friend?" demanded the sheepman truculently. "Don't you think I'm within my rights? Well, what do you mean then about following my own nature . . . are you one of these cowmen, too?"

"No," responded Hall, "I am a stranger in these parts. But after what I have seen of feuds and family wars, I should certainly hesitate to start one."

"Oh, you're a stranger, eh? Well, I believe you there . . . because any man that knows the Scarboroughs will tell you they'll never fight. You don't believe me, eh? Well, I'll see you tomorrow . . . be back with a big band of sheep . . . and, if I don't pasture them sheep in the middle of that plain, I'll buy you a ten-dollar hat."

"Very well, sir," conceded Hall, "I see you are determined. But I don't need a hat that bad."

CHAPTER NINE

The night was filled with the drumming of horses' hoofs and the rush and challenge of the hounds. They gathered by the gate and bayed and barked continuously, racing far out across the open plain, and, when at dawn the Bassetts looked out, the basin was stripped bare of stock. Not a cow or horse was left for Grimes to wreak his vengeance on if his sheep were shot up and scattered—the stage was cleared and set for the play, which promised to be a tragedy. The Bassetts peered out warily, using their glasses through the portholes as they scanned the neighboring hills for gunmen. Then the old squaw ventured out, to bring in wood and water and cook their bread and coffee on the hearth. As the sun rose higher, the oak door was thrown open, giving an unobstructed view of the plain. At last the Bassetts stepped out into the open, for the hour for ambushing had passed.

There are crimes that stalk by noonday, and others that fear the light, but the men who shoot from ambush creep up in the nighttime and kill at the first peep of day. Or, failing of their victim, they skulk off through the brush, before they, too, are marked down for revenge. All this the Bassetts knew, as well as the strange crotchet that keeps murderers from shooting down women, and so they stayed close till the hour for tapping had passed, sending their woman out instead. She plodded about stoically, apparently busy with her duties, but every possible hiding place was carefully scrutinized before she consented to let her menfolk come out.

They stood now in the sun, rolling a smoke and looking northward for the first of the four bands of sheep, and, as the clamor of their bleating came faintly down the wind, old Susie, the Indian woman, came out. First she glanced at Bill and Winchester, who were talking and laughing together, and then at sullen-faced Sharps, and then she, too, looked away to the north where the sheep were beginning to move.

"No good!" she exclaimed, stamping her foot and turning to Henry. While the other looked on, she harangued him in Indian, pointing repeatedly at her sons and the sheep. But Henry Bassett was not the man to listen to a woman when it was a question of peace or war, and after a few words he dismissed her impatiently, and joined his grinning cubs.

"She don't like that man Grimes," he explained shamefacedly, "but it's too late now for sech talk. All the same, boys, this sheep war ain't no concern of ours, so we'll stay right close to the house. I'm shore sorry now that I said what I did, because if he wins, boys, he'll sheep us out, too. But it was that or knuckle down to them bastard Scarboroughs, and I shore can't stummick that."

He maundered on, arguing it over with himself, seeking vainly to justify his acts, and all the while the braying of the sheep grew louder as the herds drifted down through the pass. For weeks they had been struggling through scrub oaks and pines, and dense thickets of manzanita and buckthorn, and, when at last they burst into the open, the leaders advanced on the run. The first band was made up of big, sturdy wethers, their fleeces torn and tattered from trailing through the brush, but strong and active as bucks. They came on in a line that quickly spread out like the front of an advancing flood, and, as the last of the herd came clear of the creekbed, the clangor of their *baaing* ceased. They fed along slowly, the leaders lingering to eat, the drag drifting past them to the front, and, in the silence that followed, a Mexican herder stepped out and looked down across the waving plain.

The grass was knee high and still green from winter rains, and it flowed away before them like a billowing field, for the sheep had never been there before. Yet this silence, this emptiness, this absence of man or beast had its sinister side as well, and, after a long look, the herder disappeared and came out farther down the creek. He kept under the bank, only showing among the shadows as he kept cover beneath the towering cottonwoods, but, as his sheep drifted away toward the grassy western hills, he rushed out and turned them back with his dogs. Still the silence, the great emptiness, and, as other herders came up, they stepped out boldly into the open. Each man carried a gun and had his face to the hills, but no gun roared out its loud challenge. They drifted on slowly, down the broadening valley yet keeping close in to the creek, and at noon they had edged away from the menacing western ridges and gained the open basin at last.

But now the fat wethers had eaten their full, and, as the heat came on, they took shelter in the river bottom, drowsing peacefully in the shade of the willows. The camp rustlers came up with their burros and kaks, a fire was soon going at their camp, and, as his burros and Mexicans took their afternoon *siesta*, Dave Grimes ambled over to the house. He rode up on a black mule, gaudy with martingale and fancy trimmings, and greeted the Bassetts at the gate.

"Well," he challenged, "didn't I tell ye I could do it? They seen my men was armed . . . and I had others to do the flanking . . . and nobody fired a shot. Now I'm out in the open, where they can't sneak up on me, and I can fight 'em man to man."

"They may not fight you that way," suggested Winchester

amiably, but the rest of the Bassetts said nothing. The sight of the sheep actually cropping off the grass that they had depended upon to pasture their horses had brought up a sober second thought, and Sharps and Bill were furious.

"What d'ye think you're going to do?" demanded Bill rebelliously, "bed your sheep down right in front of the door? We'd like a little feed where we can stake out our horses without walking plumb over to the Scarboroughs'."

"Oh, you would, hey?" returned Grimes, but there he stopped and swallowed his scathing retort. "Well, I'll speak to my herders," he said at last. "We've got to be neighborly, of course. But when I git through with 'em, you can walk to the Scarboroughs' without dodging any Forty-Five-Nineties. I see they've gathered all their cattle and drove 'em off west . . . and their gunmen are over there, too . . . but the first danged man that takes a shot at my sheep will find I've got a Forty-Five-Ninety, too. I've seen that tried before . . . riding out at my herders and jumping my sheep off some bluff . . . but I've got a way to stop it that's never failed yet. I jest give 'em a taste of this."

He patted the stock of a .45-90 rifle that stuck up from under his knee and Sharps broke his day-long silence.

"You're bad, ain't ye?" he rumbled, and Grimes saw that his new partners had already repented of their bargain.

"Yes, I'm bad," he said, "and I don't care who knows it. Anything more you'd like to say?"

"Nope," answered Sharps, and regarded him morosely, at which Grimes wheeled his mule to go.

"Well, so long," he said, "can't be chatting here all day. But if you think you're so *bravo*, why didn't you clean out them Scarboroughs yourself, without calling on me for help?"

He flashed his eyes at Sharps, and galloped over to his camp, leaving the Bassetts with something more to think about.

Why, indeed, had they brought in this barbarian with his

Mexicans and his sheep, when with a little more nerve they could have taken on the Scarboroughs and run them out of the country themselves? But it was too late now to ask that question, for Grimes and his sheep were there, and on the other hand it was too early to give way to despair, for the battle had just begun. The Scarboroughs might be cowards, but, even then, they were cowmen, and a cowardly cowman will rise up and fight sheep when he would never fight anything else. No, the battle was not over; it had not yet begun, and before he had finished, the self-satisfied Mr. Grimes might find himself hollering for help. But help he would never get, not from the Bassetts and their clan, for they had seen his raw work and he had tipped his own hand—he was there to sheep them all out!

They waited in sullen silence as the sheep began to move and the herders followed after them from the bedding ground, for that was the way these besotted sheepmen worked; they made themselves the slaves of their sheep. And the memory of that grass, so rich and sweet, had roused the sheep up early from their dreams; they set off in single file, each group behind its leader, and the leaders all heading for the plain. A single herder followed, his gun across his arm, his eyes on the distant hills, and from a knoll near their camp the extra herders watched him, for they knew he took his life in his hands. What they feared they could not say, more than the treachery of the cowmen who had disappeared so mysteriously into the hills, but they watched him nevertheless, and, as they followed his squat form, suddenly he staggered and dropped down in the grass. And then the answer came, a single shot in the silence, and the sheep broke into a run.

There was a volley then, from the rolling plain in front of them, and from a thin line of willows that marked the course of a dry stream the smoke rose up in white puffs. The sheep, which had rushed one way, now turned and rushed another, and, as they went down in sudden rows, the survivors stampeded, running frantically away from the smoke. The heavy *bang* of cowmen's rifles, shooting ninety grains of powder, added the final touch of panic to their flight, and, as they scooted across the plain, the big, .45-90-caliber bullets plowed through them until they dropped by scores. It was the vengeance of the Scarboroughs for the invading of their range, but the Bassetts did not rush for their guns. They looked on in stony silence, for it was no quarrel of theirs—and Grimes had tipped his hand too soon.

CHAPTER TEN

If Grimes had thought to win a bloodless victory and take over Maverick Basin for his sheep, he was brought back to earth by that first rifle shot, which had struck down his boldest corporal. And the fusillade that followed, killing his sheep by the hundreds and scattering them across the plain, showed the presence of an enemy as ruthless as himself and as determined to play a bold hand. No, it was too rich a prize to be given up lightly and the Scarboroughs were fighting to win. For an hour, while Grimes raged about in the distance and cursed his cowering herders, the rifle shots continued and the sorely harried sheep went down until there were no more to kill. It was a slaughter of the innocents, but each sheep that went down sent a pang through Grimes's hard heart.

The position of the Scarboroughs, behind the bank of the low creekbed that meandered across the plain, was impregnable from every side, and even after dark Grimes was afraid to venture out, lest he walk into yet another ambush. They were playing his own game—the way he had often played it when rash cowboys had charged down on his camp—and after gathering a few strays he was compelled to retreat, taking his much-vaunted Mexicans with him. Out of three thousand sheep he did not have fifty left, and his fighting corporal lay dead on the plain, shot down by a cowman's bullet.

But Grimes had made his boast that he would show the Scarboroughs, and the next morning early he came riding down the creekbed at the head of more than twenty armed Mexicans. They were ferocious-looking creatures, each armed with a rifle and a pair of .45 six-shooters, and, as they rode past the house, some charged the Bassett dogs and put them to flight with their ropes. Then they galloped on, laughing, to join Grimes and the rest, who had dismounted and tied their mules in the brush.

The Bassetts watched them through loopholes, not without muttered curses for the *bravos* who had lashed their pet hounds, but, when they saw the Mexicans start up a streambed to the west, they paused and reserved their judgment. It was the mouth of that same wash that had sheltered the ambushed Scarboroughs when they had shot down the herder and his sheep, and if the Scarboroughs were still there—they waited in tense silence, but no battle sprang up on the plain. All was quiet and still, and at last Grimes himself walked out to the body of his corporal. The Mexicans followed after him; they carried the body back, and then for a long time not a head was seen above the cutbank of the wash.

At the Rock House, far away, Hall could see through his glasses other men looking on from the mound. The Scarboroughs were at home, their horses caught and saddled, waiting to see what the next move would be. The sun mounted higher and the Bassetts stepped forth, the better to watch the grim drama, and then, from the north, there came the faint *baaa* of sheep— Grimes was throwing another herd into the basin. They came on at a trot, urged along from behind by herders and racing dogs, and, as the first band left the brush, another followed behind it, and after that a third. In long, bleating columns they strung out across the plain, heading straight for the guarded creek, and, while the Scarboroughs ran to mount, the bands swung to right and left and were held close along its bank. All three of Grimes's herds were now safely pastured in the very heart of the basin, and he and his men were between them and the Scarboroughs, securely hidden behind the cutbank of the wash. He came out into the open and held up his gun, but nobody answered the challenge.

As the Scarboroughs, the day before, had been impregnable to assault, so now Grimes held the upper hand, and, while his Mexican fighters patrolled the dry streambed, the sheep mowed down the grass. They were held in compact bands, each close to the creek, but, as no one moved against them, they were allowed to spread out and the clamor of their braying ceased. All was still in the basin—as it had been before when the first band had gone to its fate—and, as the heat came on, the sheep huddled up together and slept in each other's shade. But the Scarboroughs had disappeared, some riding south and some west, and that was a bad sign for sheep.

At the log fort of the Bassetts, they watched in patient silence, now scanning the hilltops for any signs of riding men, now turning again to the sheep. These had roused up from their drowsing and drifted out across the grasslands, anxiously guarded by three pairs of crouching herders, but, if Grimes had hoped that the Texans would charge him, he was disappointed again. They were playing a waiting game, or planning some new ambush that would mean fresh disaster to his sheep. As the afternoon wore on, Grimes scouted about uneasily, finally returning to mount his black mule. He started back toward his herds, then changed his mind suddenly, and galloped up to the Bassett door.

"What . . . hiding in the house?" he hailed in mock surprise. "You'll get white from not seeing the sun. Or . . . well, I mean no disrespect . . . but where is that man Sharps, that misdoubted I would ever win my point? Will you look out there now and see my bands of sheep, feeding along like the beauties they are? And where are the Scarboroughs that were going to wipe me out if I dared to assert my rights?"

"They're hiding in the hills," answered Winchester grimly, "and you'd better git off and come in."

"Ah, well." Grimes laughed "I see you're no great fighters or you'd be in the hills yourselves. A man must come out boldly if he expects to get his rights, but we all of us follow our own nature. And that reminds me . . . how do, Mister Hall . . . I'll be back for that ten-dollar hat!"

He turned his mule to go, looking back for the answer, and a bullet struck the ground close behind him.

"Yes, you will!" called out Bill, as the mule cringed his tail and Grimes dropped down quickly with his gun. "Git around behind the house or they'll tap you off sure . . . they're shooting from the top of that hill!"

"The damned cowards!" cursed Grimes, suddenly jumping at a close shot and dragging his mule by the head, but, as he struggled to lead it off, a third bullet came that struck the poor animal dead.

"Come in here!" yelled Winchester, throwing open the door, but Grimes had gone out of his head.

"Stay in there if you want to!" he shouted back defiantly, and started on a run for the brush. It was a scant hundred feet to the edge of the river bottom, and, as they watched him through the portholes, they saw him gliding from tree to tree, vengefully stalking the slayer of his mule. But it was far to the hilltop and before he had more than started there was a shot from out on the plain. It was answered by another, and then by a fusillade, and once more the sheep broke and ran. Who was shooting, and from where, it was impossible to say, but all the herders were gone and the Mexicans along the streambed were firing off their guns at random. The only thing that moved besides the rush of frightened sheep was Grimes, running savagely up the wash.

From the shelter of their fort, the Bassetts looked after him, and Sharps grunted scornfully to himself. But no shower of bullets followed the sheepman in his flight; he kept on and rejoined his frightened men, and, when their frantic shooting had been stilled by his boot, the old silence fell again. There was only the *skuff-skuff* of myriad feet as the sheep made a rush, then listened and rushed off again, breaking the stillness that hung over the plain. But when a hiding herder sprang up to turn them back, he went down before a single, distant shot. Then the Mexican fusillade reopened, and, when it had been silenced, the sheep were left to their fate. From the hills far away plunging shots fell among them, to add to their senseless panic, and each bullet seemed to explode, throwing up dirt and tufts of grass, making the disaster more complete.

The bulk of the herd fled back up the broad cañon and took shelter in the brush along the creek, but there once more the explosive bullets fell among them and drove them into the hills. As dusk came on, they were scattered in small bunches, hiding close, and then rushing in full flight, and, at dawn they still hid there, for Grimes's Mexicans had deserted him, thinking of nothing but to save their own lives. Three more of their number had gone down before the gun of that marksman who never missed a shot, and in the night they fled north, leaving Grimes to gather his sheep, or leave them to the wolves if he chose.

CHAPTER ELEVEN

There was a time, in the proud days of chivalry, when knights like Sir Lancelot had to ride forth disguised in order to tempt others to fight, but all this was changed when Colonel Colt and his six-shooter reduced men to about the same size. Dave Grimes had ridden in and challenged the Scarboroughs to fight him, to come out and battle for their range, but they had taken a leaf from his own book of warfare and kept under cover like Indians. Not for them the bold charge, the midnight raid on armed camps; they gave him his head until they had him where they wanted him, and then shot his Mexicans from ambush. Four men had been struck dead, and even then the wary Scarboroughs had kept beyond the range of his guns. They were playing safe, a hundred percent safe, and Grimes threw up his hands and quit.

Of the ten thousand sheep, worth $5 apiece, that he had driven in to eat out their range, he took back a thousand or fifteen hundred at the most, leaving the rest to the mercy of the wolves. He was broken, beaten, but as he looked back across the basin, he shook his grimy fist and swore vengeance. He had left their valley with a stench from the bodies of sheep, and three herders lay unburied on the plain, but, as he retreated up the cañon, he sent word to the Scarboroughs that they should pay for their killings, and more.

They watched him from the ridges until he was well on his way, and then headed back toward the store, riding down the valley at a gallop and shooting off their pistols while they whooped their derision at the Bassetts. There were drinks, and more drinks, and wild rides across the battlefield, while the Bassetts looked on somberly. A great peril had been lifted, the sheep were gone, but now they were at the mercy of this band of drunken Texans who might any time charge down on their house. Or slip up in the nighttime, like the skulkers they were, and shoot them down at dawn! Even Bill was quiet and old Susie muttered as she gazed across the plain at their enemies. The Scarboroughs were so many and they were so few—but old Henry refused to be alarmed.

The day wore on, and, as the revelry became wilder, a messenger rode over with his hand up for peace and handed the Bassetts a note. Sharps gazed at it blankly and passed it to Bill, who passed it along to Winchester.

"Says here," he read, " 'take your black squaw and go, you dirty sons-of-bitches.' Well, that's enough for me. Who gave you that?" he demanded of the startled neutral, and the messenger wheeled his horse.

"Isham Scarborough," he replied, and was starting to go when Winchester beckoned him back.

"What's your rush?" he asked. "Can't you wait for the answer? Well, you tell Isham Scarborough that I'll shoot him on sight . . . and that goes for Red and Elmo. And you tell the three Scarboroughs, if they'll ride out halfway, we'll meet 'em on horseback . . . with six-shooters. Can you keep that from rattling around in your head?"

"Why, y-yes!" stuttered the neutral, and went galloping back, while the Bassetts ran for their horses.

"That sheepman was right, boys," observed Winchester soberly, as they sat mounted and waiting to go. "If we'd had the nerve, we'd've done this long ago and never have called him in. He's gone now, thank God, and we're back to where we started from, but you know them Scarboroughs . . . we're next."

"Yes, you're right, Son," quavered old Henry, "they're dead set ag'in' us . . . they're determined to wipe us out. I've allus been peaceable, but a man must protect himself, only don't take no chances with Isham. You head for him first, Winchester, and let Sharps take on Red, and Bill can shore clean up on Elmo."

"Yes, you bet I can," cursed Bill, "but the cowardly whelp is fixing to ride back home."

"They're all going," growled Sharps, and reined his horse out the gate. "Come on," he said, "let's rush 'em!"

"Nope," vetoed old Henry, "you want to be keerful, boys, and remember your old dad and mammy. Jest ride out slow and hold up your guns, and, if they don't come out, they're cowards."

"No use," grumbled Winchester as the Scarboroughs galloped off, "you couldn't make that outfit fight. But, come on, boys, anyway, let's go over to the store and lay in a little grub and tobacco."

"I'll go with you," spoke up Hall, who had been chafing for action, and he swung up on his waiting roan.

"Well, all right." Winchester smiled. "You seem to be willing, if you ain't drawing a gunman's pay. And anything we can do for you. . . ."

"Don't mention it," shot back Hall, and they rode off together, for already they had come to be friends.

The trail to the store was encumbered with dead sheep that already had drawn flocks of crows, and, as they rose up, *cawing*, Hall had a vision of a picture he had once seen of war. Here was the same grim battlefield, only the victims were sheep, and there, riding off, was the horde of barbarians who had left such ruin in their wake. They strung off across the basin, and, well up in the lead, Hall could see the buckskin pony of Meshacka-tee. Since he had quit the arrogant Scarboroughs, he had had his misgivings about Meshackatee, for he knew he stood high in their counsels, and he wondered whether this slaughter of Mexican herders and their sheep were not the result of his wiles.

He was a shrewd man, Meshackatee, and he had admitted himself that he was doing the heavy thinking for the gang. But would he now consent to turn these Indian tactics against old Henry Bassett and his sons? Hall was loath to believe it, and yet he was not sure, for Meshackatee had a strange sense of loyalty. He called himself a hired *bravo*, and then in the next breath he said that no man could buy him. He would think what he pleased; only as long as he took Scarborough money did he feel he owed Isham his service. And Meshackatee had made a bargain with Hall, that circumstances had soon brought to nothing, but Hall still wondered if Meshackatee understood, for he had favored Hall with a sly wink at parting. Was it not possible, even yet, that Meshackatee considered him a spy, and his joining the Bassetts a mere blind, and that perhaps already Allifair was waiting to greet him, when he should return and bring his news? He gazed at the huge form on the distant buckskin horse and shook his head sadly.

Right or wrong, he had thrown in his lot with the Bassetts, and, if it came to a fight, he would feel it his duty to protect them against all aggression, and yet—the days were longer than any he had known and the watches of the night were endless. He could see her through his glasses when he watched the far Rock House, this woman whose heart had remained faithful to his memory when she had given him up for dead. Was it right, after all, for him to follow his conscience when it left her to work like a slave? And could he not, in a pinch, turn upon the savage Sharps and so gain his freedom once more? But, no, he could never meet Isham again without shooting it out then and there. They were born to be enemies, to oppose each other to the end, and he had crossed his Rubicon when he had slapped Isham in the face and called him a coward and a fool.

There was no one at the store but the weak-eyed Mr. Johnson and a group of staring neutrals, but the bottles were everywhere and several of the settlers were drunker than strict neutrality called for. The Bassetts rode up slowly, scanning every face in the slack crowd, and, while the others went in, Sharps stood by, outside the door, to be ready for any treachery.

"Gimme five dollars worth of smoking tobacco," began Winchester peremptorily, "and we want to git an order of grub."

"Why, yes . . . certainly," cringed Johnson, starting to get it, and then drawing back, "but . . . *er* . . . I'm sorry, but the Scarboroughs have forbidden me. . . ."

"I'm talking to you!" rasped Winchester, and there was a moment of silence as the meaning of his statement went home.

"But they said they'd come back," protested Johnson in desperation, "and tear down my store if I did!"

"I'll tear it down right now," answered Winchester, "if you don't shell out that grub."

The storekeeper shelled out, but he showed a mean spirit and Winchester tapped on the counter with his gun.

"Mister Johnson," he said, "have you joined the Scarborough gang? Oh, you ain't, eh? You're a neutral. Well, try to act the part then, or we'll come over and clean you out. Good day . . . and keep your mouth shut."

They rode back heavily laden with supplies and tobacco, for the Bassetts looked forward to a siege, but no siege came, and they went to slaughtering hogs, oblivious of the Scarboroughs' threat. It was Winchester who took the lead, for the banter of the sheepman had stung him to the quick, and day or night he rode forth boldly, gathering horses or riding to his hounds. If old Henry disapproved, he did nothing to show it, and Bill and Sharps worked on stoically, but the Indian woman sat where she could always see the hills, and Hall watched the Rock House through his glasses.

A week went by and no storm broke upon them; the Scarboroughs had gone west to work their cattle. Then in the night Hall heard the hounds rush out, and a woman's voice called for help. The Bassetts sprang up and ran to their loopholes, for their first thought was always of treachery, but Hall recognized the voice and rushed out through the doorway, striking the hounds aside as he ran.

"Allifair!" he cried, gathering her close into his arms and lifting her up from the dogs, and, as the Bassetts stood staring, he carried her into the house while the hounds followed meekly behind.

CHAPTER TWELVE

She had stood trembling and holding close to him, her eyes on the swarthy Bassetts and the old squaw who was stirring up the fire, but when they had retired and left the lovers to themselves, Allifair whispered swift words into Hall's ears.

"They're coming," she warned. "I know it for a certainty, because Meshackatee told me himself. And they're going to kill all the Bassetts."

He gripped her and sat still, his eyes on the weak blaze that was lapping the black stones of the fireplace, and then he inclined his head. The Bassett boys were near, lying stolidly on their beds, which they had dragged back a little into the darkness, but he knew that some of them were listening. The jealous-eyed Sharps had never ceased to watch him since the day he had come to the house, and, seeing him now with this niece of the Scarboroughs, his ears would be straining for every word.

"They're strangers," she whispered, "some Slashknife men that Isham sent out for and hired secretly. And when they ride up and catch the Bassetts off their guard, they're to draw their guns and shoot."

He gripped her again, for she was whispering too loudly—or so it seemed to his jangled nerves—and then he sat waiting in the silence. It pressed in upon him, as oppressive as the darkness, as fearful as the thoughts it brought up, and the stir of their breathing, even the beating of their hearts took on a terrible distinctness. But her message was not finished, and, as he held her close, she whispered very softly in his ear.

"We must go," she said. "He told me to tell you. He'll be waiting with horses . . . down the creek."

He nodded, and his mind slipped back into the past, and then leaped forward to the future. In a whirlwind of dancing visions he pictured their flight down the dark cañon, and Meshackatee waiting with the horses, and then his mind struck back and he could see the Bassetts, and the Slashknife men riding in. He imagined their short parley, the secret signal, the flash of guns, and then these men who lay about him now would be shot down and left like the sheepherders.

"I can't leave," he whispered back. "I've got to stay and help them. But you. . . ."

She clutched him again and was whispering earnestly into his ear when Sharps rose up from his bed. It was just a fold of blankets, laid down on the dirt floor, and, as he rose, Bill rose up, too.

"What are you folks whispering about?" demanded Sharps, advancing in his stocking feet from the gloom, and Winchester sat up suddenly.

"Oh, you mustn't tell," pleaded Allifair frantically. "I promised him I wouldn't, you know."

"Promised who?" inquired Sharps, and, as she shrank away from him, Hall laid a soothing hand on her head.

"She came," he said, "to deliver me a message . . . a friend has offered to help us escape. We were engaged to be married and I came up here to find her, but she has been held a kind of prisoner at the Rock House."

"Yes," challenged Sharps, still unconvinced, "but didn't I hear her say that someone was coming to kill the Bassetts?"

"You bet you did," put in Bill, "because I heard it myself. This here don't look good to me."

"If you gentlemen will just step back," suggested Hall quietly, "and let us talk this over a minute. . . ."

"All right," spoke up Winchester, coming quickly to the front, "get back, boys. We know he's our friend."

"Well, I don't," grumbled Sharps, but he made room, reluctantly, when Winchester shoved him away. They gathered in a knot in the back part of the room, arguing angrily among themselves, while Hall talked in low tones with Allifair.

"I am in honor bound to stay," he ended gently, "so you will have to go back . . . and wait."

"What . . . back to the Rock House?" she protested indignantly. "And leave you here to be killed. No, Hall, I am going to stay."

"Well, that is your right," he responded after a silence. "God knows I'll protect you, if I can. How many did you say there were?"

"Oh, were you going to fight them? Why not leave it to . . . ? But, no, I know you too well. There are eight or ten of them, Hall."

"And since your life and mine are involved in it now. . . ."

"You can tell them," she consented, and sighed.

The Bassetts listened grimly as he told the brief story of Isham and his Slashknife killers, and then Winchester held out his hand.

"Don't you worry," he said, with a smile to Allifair, "we'll take care of you, lady . . . and him. All we needed was to know their little game."

He stepped out jauntily as he laid her a bed by the fire, and then took his brothers outside. What he said Hall never knew, but when they came back, even Sharps had a friendly smile.

They slept till daylight—or lay in their blankets—and at dawn there was a man at every loophole, searching the country for the first sight of the gunmen. The sun was just up when they appeared in the north, riding down the Turkey Creek trail, but, as they left the brush, two men fell behind and disappeared in the creekbed.

"One of them fellers was Red," announced Bill, who was looking through the glasses. "I'd know that wool hat of his anywhere. There's eight of 'em now, altogether."

"Let me look!" demanded Winchester, and, after peering through the porthole, he passed the glasses to Sharps.

"All *Tejanos*," he said. "Well, boys, this means business, and we might as well shoot to kill. I'll meet 'em at the door, and, when they go for their guns . . . well, you know, don't wait too long."

Sharps grunted and caught up his rifle impatiently. Bill watched them as they rode down the valley, and, when they turned off and took the trail to their house, he, too, dropped down by a porthole. As for Hall, he led Allifair to old Susie's room and leaned his carbine against the left side of the door. This opened to the right, as most doors do, and there was a niche that just hid the gun.

"What's the idee?" inquired Winchester with the old, carefree smile that seemed to come to him in moments of danger, and Hall smiled back, although soberly.

"I'm left-handed," he explained, "that is, with a rifle . . . with a pistol I use the right hand. Well, they'll be watching my right hand, but I'll reach in with my left and have my carbine before they know it."

"And then . . . ?" prompted Winchester, but Hall only shrugged and glanced back significantly at Allifair. Already she had left the room in the rear and was looking on with growing alarm—for the horses were outside the door. There was a rush of hounds, a curse and a yelp, and then a voice hailed the house.

"Well?" inquired Winchester, opening the door about a foot and looking them over coldly, and the leader of the cowboys spoke roughly.

"We're lost," he said, "been riding all night. What's the

chances for something to eat?"

"I guess you've come to the wrong house," returned Winchester politely. "That's the Scarborough place over there."

He opened the door and pointed off across the plain, but the Texans were not to be denied. They were Texans, every one, and there was a wild look in their eyes as they reined in their horses and sat, waiting. Winchester noted it, but his manner was calm.

"Well, all right," he said, when they protested ignorance of the Scarboroughs, "we ain't running no restaurant, but if you'll wait outside a while. . . ."

"Outside?" snapped the leader, quick to snatch at some offense, and his men ranged in behind him.

"We have ladies in the house," explained Winchester, still suavely, and Allifair appeared behind him.

"Well, tell 'em to come out," ordered the boss cowboy threateningly, "and git us something to eat!"

"Take her away," whispered Hall, brushing Winchester aside and stepping in front of Allifair. "Good morning, gentlemen," he said. "I hope you'll excuse us. . . ."

"Send the women out!" snarled the cowboy, glaring at Hall in a fury. "You'd better, if you know what's good for you."

"What do you mean?" demanded Hall, and, as Winchester came back and stood in the door, the killer gave the signal to shoot.

"We have a way," he announced, "of getting what we want!" And he laid his hand on his gun.

He was quick, but Hall was quicker—his hand snatched out the rifle and he shot from the hip at the leader. Then, as the cowboys drew their pistols, he plunged into the midst of them, shooting right and left with his carbine. There was a fusillade of pistol shots, the *bang* of rifles from loopholes, and, as the horses pitched and jostled, three men fell down between them and were trampled in the wild stampede. The horses did the rest—

84

they bolted to escape the shooting and their riders soon gave them their heads. It was a rout, but the Bassetts had gone out of their heads with rage and the lust for blood. They had turned berserk in a moment, and, as the Texans galloped away, they shot two more off their horses. Of the three men who were left, two took to the creek bottom and the other dropped down behind his horse.

"Leave him to me!" ordered Winchester, stepping out into the open, and the killer grabbed for his gun. It was on the wrong side, the one toward the house, and, as he reached under his horse's neck, Winchester shot at his head and clipped off a part of one ear. The killer jerked back and reached over his horse's neck, only to receive another wound in the arm.

"Get away from that horse!" shouted Winchester fiercely, and then shot it through and through. The killer turned and fled, his broken arm flapping, and the Bassetts let him go. They had had their fill of killing and blood, for three men lay dead in the yard. Of the two wounded who escaped, one was never seen again, and the other, fleeing north, encountered a she bear with cubs, which mangled him so that he died. Only two escaped unhurt, to return to the Slashknife and tell of the man-killing Bassetts.

CHAPTER THIRTEEN

As in desert spaces, the bodies of the dead draw vultures from hundreds of miles, so the news of the battle, spread by some mysterious means, brought the neutrals to the scene of the killing. They came from distant cañons, from up under the Mogollon Rim, and from the west as far as Clear Creek, and, as they gazed at the dead cowboys, they muttered among themselves and glanced at the Bassetts, and Hall. There was awe and wonder—and a new respect—in their eyes, for each man had been shot stone dead. Two in the heart and one through the brain, and the horses had been bucking like broncos. That was shooting—and done by the Bassetts.

The story of Winchester's duel passed from lip to lip—how he had put an underbit in Tucker's left ear and broken his arm when he reached over. It was he who had shot Paine through the heart, unless the stranger, Hall, had beat him to it, and Bill and Sharps probably had got the rest, because the wounds had all been made with a rifle. And so these were the half Indians that the Scarboroughs had been so scornful of and had called the dirty black sons-of-bitches. They gazed and rode home, and their neighbors returned just to look at the fighting Bassetts. Then they gathered at the store, and what they said there was carried to the crestfallen Scarboroughs.

No longer did they dare to ride over to the store and buy the drinks for their gunmen, and the neutrals. A wave of resentment had been roused up against them by the exposure of their treacherous plan, and they kept close to the Rock House and waited. But they were far from being whipped, and, when Hall spoke of leaving, he was warned that they were watching the trails. So he lingered on from day to day, hardly noticing the passage of time as he talked of the future with Allifair. But though she smiled bravely and agreed to all his plans, she had caught a trick from the watchful old squaw, and, whether they strolled beneath the cottonwoods or rode out across the plain, her eyes were always straying to the hills. Perhaps it was presentiment, a premonition of coming bloodshed—or perhaps, having lived with the Scarboroughs so long, she sensed what was going on—and each day she grew more watchful, more apprehensive of danger, although she passed it off with a smile.

As she would go through the doorway, she would glance instinctively at the bullet holes where the Slashknife men had shot up the house, and the dark, bloody stains where three men had died would send a shudder through her body as she passed. Old memories leaped up of other days when her own kinsmen had been shot down at their doors, and when the man at her side had come prowling back at night to shoot down even more. He had killed her own kin, and her brothers had killed his, and now, like a nightmare, another feud rose to thwart them, for the Scarboroughs would shoot him on sight. For it was Hall, leaping out into the midst of the killers, who had defeated them by spoiling their aim, and she, by running away and revealing the plot, had added fresh fuel to their hate. But they would not kill her—even the Scarboroughs had their shame—all they would do would be to shoot down her lover. And so she waited, and trembled.

For a week and more the Bassetts had kept close, sensing the mischief in the air, but, as the days wore by and the Scarboroughs did not strike, their vigilance at last relaxed. None of the Scarboroughs had been killed; it was not a blood feud yet, but only some sheepherders on the side of the Bassetts and some cowboys employed by the Scarboroughs. The old enmity remained and the Scarboroughs were implacable, but the Bassetts were still for peace. They had proved their worth as fighting men *par excellence* and were content to let sleeping dogs lie. So, as all remained quiet, Winchester rode out across the range, and the next day was Sharps's turn to go.

There had been rain during the night and the morning was crystal clear; all the hills stood out clean against the sky, and, as the sun rose up higher without revealing any ambush, the men took their ropes and stepped out. It was Sharps who went first, heading straight across the flat to where his night horse was circling its stake, and Winchester and Bill had started after him when something called them back. Hall ventured forth last of all, for Allifair had delayed him, and halfway to his horse she called him again. He turned, but too late—there was a volley from the hills and he and Sharps went down.

There was a silence, an aching moment when even the horses stood still, and then, as Allifair sprang out to run to Hall, a strong hand hurled her back. The door slammed behind her, and, as the bar fell in place, she heard Winchester's voice in the darkness.

"It's them Scarboroughs!" he cursed. "Don't you step outside the door or they'll shoot you down like a dog. Bill, take that far loophole . . . they're up on this first hill . . . and, Dad, you watch the door."

He fumbled for his gun and hurried off to guard a porthole, and old Henry took his post by the door. Within the darkened house there was silence again, except for the wailing of Susie and the muttering of the startled men. They had been taken by surprise, and, as they scanned the empty landscape, they imagined enemies springing up everywhere. Bill watched the creekbed and Winchester the south hill, and old Henry, his voice plaintive, gave way to senile laments as he gazed at the body of Sharps.

"He's . . . he's alive, boys," he quavered, as he saw the huge bulk move, and, before they could stop him, he had unbarred the door and dashed out into the open. The assassins on the hilltop seemed to hesitate from shame, or perhaps they were waiting to make sure, but as he passed out the gate, a heavy rifle roared and the old man tottered and fell.

"Come back here!" shouted Winchester, snatching Allifair as she fled, and, while he was dragging her back, old Susie eluded him and ran screaming to bring in her husband. He had risen on his knees, but, as she stooped to lift him up, a second bullet, aimed deadly straight, almost tore him from her arms. Old Henry was struck dead, but she would not believe it; she dragged him back anyway, crying out against his murderers, while the men on the hilltop laughed.

"That's three of 'em!" they yelled, and Winchester barred the door again, for he feared that his mother would be next. The Scarboroughs had come to make good their boast and kill the last of the Bassetts, and the old Indian woman was no more to them than one of the barking dogs. They had come to kill them all, and even the gentle Allifair could not pass out that door and come back. They were killers, after all, these cowardly Scarboroughs, but killers in their own way, the sneaking, stealthy way of the Apaches who hunted men down like game. Three men already had fallen before their guns, and Winchester knew them; they would not fight in the open. They would not rush the house, and, while Bill kept a look-out, Winchester stood with his hand on the door.

Outside, on the plain, Hall McIvor lay limply where he had dropped at the first fatal volley, but Sharps, groaning and grunting like a huge, wounded bear, was clawing the earth with his hands. He did not call out, but inched feebly toward the house, and Winchester turned away. The men on the hill were letting Sharps live in order to trap both him and Bill, for before they could reach Sharps, the Scarboroughs would shoot them down, and then they would finish him. It was a part of their system, figured out to a nicety, but Winchester and Bill did not go out. They stayed by their loopholes, searching the hilltop for some movement that would reveal the cunning ambush of the enemy.

The sun had become hot and Sharps sank back exhausted; his black head heaved, and he was dead. Of all the Bassetts, the Scarboroughs had feared him most, and now that he was gone, they hooted. Winchester and Bill, by their loopholes inside the house, still watched the hillside, so ominously barren of life, but not a man moved, and they did not fire a cartridge, for they would need them all, if they lived. They were outnumbered and surrounded, and, when night fell, their enemies would creep down close. They would slip up to the house, which two men could not guard, and fire it or break down the door, and then the Bassetts, if they lived that long, might hope to avenge their dead.

In the corner old Susie sat swaying back and forth while she mourned over the body of her husband, and at the loophole by the door Allifair gazed out through her tears at the form that had once been her lover. He lay on his face in a shallow hole, where the hogs in rooting had dug out a wallow in a slight depression in the ground. Her first madness was gone now and she knew better than to go near him, for before she could rush out and bring in his body, they would riddle it again with bullets. It was better to wait, although it wrung her heart to do so, until night should bring its black shroud, and then she could go forth and take him in her arms and weep out the anguish in her breast.

She closed her eyes in prayer—although for what she did not know, since all that she lived for was lost—but, as she looked out again, she thought she saw his body move, his hand draw slowly back! She stepped to the door, which had been barred against her, and pulled it open to see. Yes, his body had moved, but at the snouting of a huge hog that even now was grunting in his face.

With a cry she flung the heavy door wide open and dashed out to save his dear body. To be mangled by hogs, and within sight of she who loved him—her anger swept her forth before she knew it. So swiftly did she run that she had reached down and caught him up before the first shot rang out, and, knowing their purpose, she shielded him with her body while the bullets smashed spitefully all about her. They were trying to frighten her, to make her drop her burden or expose him to a last vengeful shot, but the blood of Southern feudists ran strong in her veins, and she faced the hill disdainfully. Then, as she gathered him closer and started for the house, the storm of bullets ceased. Winchester and Bill had marked down their men and their rifles were clearing the hill.

She dragged him through the doorway and sank down, half fainting—and, when she came to, he was alive. Alive and standing, although with grim lines about his mouth and a terrible intentness in his eyes.

"My sweetheart," he murmured, stooping to kiss her once more, and then he lifted her up. Yes, her lover who had been dead, had come back to life, to cherish and protect her still, and, asking no questions, she drew down his head and tried to kiss the anger from his eyes.

CHAPTER FOURTEEN

There is a look in the eyes of eagles that sometimes is found in men—a bold, resolute look, changing swiftly to defiance and a hatred that nothing can quench. It is the sign of the fighting man—not the sly, vicious killer, but the man who will fight till he dies. Hall McIvor had worn it blazingly when he reached for his rifle and strode over to join the Bassetts.

"Played 'possum, eh?" muttered Winchester, who had lost his old smile. "Well, I wish we could bring in Sharps."

"No use," answered Hall, "they're just waiting to get you. Shall I kill the rest of those hogs?"

"Yes, kill the last one of them!" burst out Winchester in a frenzy. "My God, them Scarboroughs ain't human!"

"No, they're not," replied Hall, and glanced up at the hill before he crossed the room to attend to the hogs. He surveyed them with loathing, with a shudder of horror at the fate he had so narrowly missed, and then, very carefully, he shot them one by one as they gathered about the body of Sharps. They followed their own nature, even as the men upon the hill, and so he shot them down, and so he would shoot—and without any more remorse—the men who had ambushed Sharps. Their bullets had gone wild or they would have shot him, too, and left him a carcass for the hogs, and, but for the devotion of the woman that he loved, he would be at their mercy still.

At the first volley of shots he had known that he was caught, and that to run was to invite certain death, and so he had dropped down, rolling swiftly out of sight while the smoke was still in their eyes. It was a trick that he had learned from the same careful father who had reared him with but one object in life—to make him a killer of men, a terror to the Randolph clan. He it was who had taught him to shoot left-handed with the rifle, since then he would present his right side to the enemy and avoid a fatal bullet through the heart. But in the battle a bullet had found his guarded heart; he had been left on the field for dead, and now, a second time, he had been spared from death in order to live for revenge.

They still thought he was dead, those whooping cravens on the hillside who had seen him dragged into the house, but, if there was a God above to look down and judge men's hearts, he swore to make them pay. Not while he could lift a hand should they shoot down white-haired men and make sport of weeping women; they had invited the wrath of Almighty God and he would be His sure sword. His hand, which they thought dead, should rise and smite them; he would kill them one by one. He paused, for Allifair had laid her hand on his and was gazing deep down into his eyes.

"Remember," she said, "you are mine now. I saved you. And we must leave this horrible place."

He frowned and drew back, a stern refusal on his lips as he remembered the pitiless code of the feudist—but at the look in her eyes he bowed his head and gave her his hand in assent.

"It is the only way," she whispered, "if we are ever to end the feud before all our kinfolk are dead. Let these men fight it out. But if you join in with them now, I know you, you will never draw out. Let Winchester and Bill take their revenge on the Scarboroughs, and we will go back home. They cannot kill us then, because I shall be a McIvor and you will have married a Randolph."

"Yes, dear." He nodded, but he would not say more, and she

left him to watch over the dead.

The long day dragged on with men shouting from the hilltops, and then the smash and thud of the big, explosive bullets announced the beginning of a new attack. In some way the Scarboroughs had procured bullets that blew up the instant they struck against the house, and at each volley of shots the mortised logs crashed and jumped, while the chinks gave off a thin smoke. But after the first volleys, the shooting died away and again a voice shouted from the hill. Hall muttered—it was the voice of Isham.

"Hey! Send out that woman!" he called down loudly. "Last chance! We're going to do a clean job!"

"Yes you are!" yelled back Bill, but Winchester was silent and it remained for Hall to speak.

"You'd better go, Allifair," he said. "I'll try to join you later." And then he whispered a few last words into her ear.

"Dare to trust 'em?" questioned Winchester as Hall opened the door, and, when Hall nodded, he assented. "Well, good bye, then," he said, giving his hand to Allifair, "I'll see that Mister Hall gets away."

"Oh, will you?" she cried, and glanced guiltily at her lover, then gave the haggard Winchester both her hands. But there was something more, and, as she gazed at him inquiringly, he reached down and picked up a blanket. "For him," he said, and, glancing out at Sharps, he turned and strode abruptly away. Then she knew and the tears started suddenly to her eyes as she stepped bravely out into the open.

"Go back to the Rock House!" directed Isham from his hiding place, but she went past the body of Sharps. Hall watched her as she bent down and covered it up without even a glance at the hill, and, as she went across the plain, he followed her through his glasses, although the bullets were smashing against the house. As each ball struck, it seemed to rend the timbers, spitting lead viciously in through the chinks, and once more old Susie raised her voice in a wail, for she knew that the end was near. While the sun was in the sky, Winchester could keep them at bay, but when the shadows fell and blurred his sights, then the Scarboroughs would come down from their hill. They would creep up to the house and throw fire on the roof and shoot them all down as they ran, and the body of her husband would be burned where it lay—the Scarboroughs would destroy them all. But Winchester had taken the shovel from the fireplace and started a hole under the wall, and, as evening came on, he buckled on his two six-shooters and stepped to the mouth of his tunnel.

"Well, boys," he said, "we've got to skip out or they'll burn the old woman's house. I'm heading south, myself, as soon as it gets dark, and Bill, you'd better head north. Don't no one come near me, because I'm going to run hog wild and shoot at every bush I see move. You stay right here, Hall, until the fireworks begin, and then give the lady my regards. If I git out of this alive, I'll take care of them Scarboroughs without any assistance from you."

He shook hands with them gravely and dropped down into the hole; they heard him digging, and then he was gone. Bill wriggled out after him, bellying off through the weeds, and Hall watched from the bottom of the hole.

Already the evening star was glowing in the west and the dusk gathered deeper among the trees; every shadow veiled some movement; the very earth seemed to whisper and the wind rustled by like a snake. He started and crouched back as he heard a shot up the creek, then three more, and a racing through the brush, but still he held back until, down toward the south, the night suddenly burst into flame. There were shouts and loud challenges, a running fusillade that led away rapidly around the hill, and then, like a shadow, he glided out of his hiding place and disappeared in the river bottom below.

A half hour later, riding a Scarborough horse that he had stolen from its picket on the plain, he circled around and edged in on the Rock House, where the dogs were baying like mad.

Along the hillside to the east the fight was still raging, breaking out after a short silence in a sudden rattle of pistol shots, punctuated by the *bang* of heavy rifles. Winchester had carried the war into the Scarborough camp, and, knowing every man for his enemy, he had set them all to shooting by the swiftness with which he moved. When they were not firing at him, they were firing at each other, and from the Indian mound, where he had agreed to meet Allifair, Hall could see that they were scattered everywhere. Fights were springing up like wildfire, only to die down suddenly after a veritable blaze of shooting, and in his manhunter's mind he saw the wisdom of Winchester's move in going among them alone. But he had come to find Allifair and hurry her away before the Scarboroughs returned from their siege, and, standing beneath the oak tree, where she could just see him against the sky, he looked across the creek at the house.

It was dark, except for a dim light in the kitchen, and against the square doorway he could see women's forms as they hastened to and fro. And a woman's voice, loud, scolding and insistent, made known the presence of the vixenish Miz Zoolah. At long intervals, as he listened, he could hear the voice of Allifair as she attempted some faint defense, and then Miz Zoolah would burst out afresh as she hurried out to listen to the shooting.

"I hope he kills them all!" she railed from the doorway. "Yes, and leaves them lay for the hogs!" She dodged into the house to renew her loud scolding and Hall settled down to wait. From the loophole in her kitchen Allifair could look out and see him, dimly outlined beneath the branches of the tree, but she could not come out until the battle was ended and Miz Zoolah had retired to her rest. From the bunkhouse beyond and around the lighted kitchen, the watchdogs still bayed at the east, but no messenger came to bring news of the fighting and Mrs. Scarborough lingered on and on. At last the shooting stopped and the hounds challenged a galloping rider, who stayed to eat, and then spurred away. As midnight approached, the house quieted down and a form came silently up the path.

It was Allifair, her few clothes tied up in a bundle, turning nervously to look back at the house. As Hall rose to meet her, she ran to his arms and burst into long-repressed tears.

"Oh, that woman," she sobbed, "if she wasn't my own aunt. . . ." And then she fell to weeping. "But anyway," she went on, "Bill and Winchester got away, and two or three men got shot. They're looking for them everywhere, and I suppose the trails will be watched . . . do you think we can get past their guards?"

"We can try," answered Hall, "that is, if you wish. But perhaps it would be better if I came back for you later, when the excitement has kind of died down. You could hardly stand the journey now. This day has been too much."

"Yes, it has," she acknowledged, sinking down on the ground and pillowing her head against his breast, "and yet . . . we are always putting it off. Back home we could have married, but you had to build our cabin first, and now . . . well, where could we go?"

"I don't know," answered Hall, "because I'm a stranger in this country. I only know one trail out. And that trail will be guarded. So perhaps, after all. . . ."

"But you'll come back soon, won't you?" she murmured wearily. "I'm afraid I can't go now. The strain was too much for me, when I thought you were dead . . . something seemed to snap in my brain. But now, listen, dear, please don't join in this fighting. Will you always remember me first? And think of our kinsfolk back there in Kentucky . . . and of all our happiness, too. Think how happy we could be if we were married at last and back in our own mountains again, and the Randolphs and McIvors, after all these years. . . ."

She stopped and sat bolt upright, a nervous tremor running through her, for Mrs. Scarborough had risen up before them. She held a pistol in one hand and behind her followed a dog that bristled at Hall and growled.

"Put up those hands!" she commanded, pointing her pistol at him threateningly. "And so you're Hall McIvor! Well, let me tell you, Mister McIvor, your father killed my brother and he killed my sister's son, too. You're nothing but a murderer, and, if you make the least move, I'm going to shoot you dead. And before I'll let Allifair marry a son of Bland McIvor, I'll shoot her down in her tracks!"

She towered above them, like a witch in the starlight, and, as Allifair broke down and gave way to tears, Hall lifted her up gently.

"You don't need that pistol," he said to Miz Zoolah, "because no man that claims to be a gentleman ever raised his hand against a woman. I never have, and I never will."

"Yes, there you go again," she burst out vindictively. "I ought to have known it was you. Was there ever a McIvor that didn't have the same twaddle about his honor, and being a gentleman? Well, what kind of honor is it when a grown man like your father shoots down my sister's boy? He was just a child, hardly fourteen years old."

"Yes, but he shot at my father twice. And a boy, Missus Scarborough, can pull just as hard on a trigger as a man that's forty years old."

"Well, if that isn't a McIvor!" she burst out, laughing spitefully, "but I'll fix you, here and now. You put that fool down and march back to the house. I'll turn you over to Isham."

"You know he'll kill me," replied Hall, suddenly stepping away from Allifair, and Miz Zoolah raised her voice.

"Yes, and I'll kill you," she yelled, "you miserable murderer! Go on, now . . . step off down that path!"

He hesitated, for his hot Southern blood was up, and Allifair sprang at her aunt.

"Run!" she cried, striking the gun aside, and Hall made a jump into the darkness. The dog, which had been watching him, rushed in and grabbed his leg, but Hall turned and kicked him off, and, as Miz Zoolah began to shoot, he plunged down the hill and was gone.

CHAPTER FIFTEEN

When a man flees for safety, it is seldom into the unknown, for that is always fearful. Nine times out of ten he heads for some old stamping ground, and generally he heads for home. Hall McIvor was lost in a country so wild that not even a wagon track entered it; four trails led in and out, and he took the one he knew, the one that went to Tonto. It was night, but he had a horse that knew the way, or at least that could follow a trail, and at the first flush of dawn he spurred down Jump-Off Point and splashed into Turkey Creek. Then he rode without stopping until, at Cold Spring, his horse threw up its head and quit. Hall was back where his troubles had begun.

At this same spot, not a month before, Isham Scarborough and Red had held him up and charged him with being a Bassett. Now the month had passed and he was a Bassett, and the Scarboroughs would be hot on his trail. If they caught him again, the hangman's knot in the cliff-dwelling would be something more than a grim joke. The Scarboroughs were desperate; they had tried to kill off the Bassetts as they would stamp out a nest of rattlesnakes, but the most dangerous one had escaped, leaving his mark on three of them, and they would ride like the wind to cut him off. And, next after Winchester and the impetuous Bill, they would seek for Hall McIvor. Miz Zoolah would see to that, now that she knew he was Allifair's lover, and Isham would shoot him on sight. He looked around anxiously, casting about for some hiding place, and his eyes came to rest on a cliff-dwelling.

It was stuck like a swallow's nest in a hole in the rocks, high up against the base of the crag, and there, although he would have neither food nor water, he would find shelter from his enemies. For that very purpose the ancient cliff-dwellers had built it there, and every steep trail and closely built rampart had been constructed with the idea of defense. Yet if he left his horse below, they would know he was hiding near and hunt him down like a rabbit—he mounted again and spurred on down the trail until once more he came to the creek. There he loosened the horse's saddle and set him free, stepping off into the running water.

The trail itself had struck over a long point that came down from Baker Mountain to the west and he turned up the creek-bed, stepping from stone to stone, until he had made his way back to Cold Spring. Then he waded up the torrent that rushed down from the cliffs, and, as he ducked under the wild grapevines, his feet fell into a natural pathway, worn deep along the sides of the chasm. It was an ancient trail, half obliterated by cloudbursts and the rush of tumbling waters, but, as it led up higher and the chasm widened out, Hall had a feeling that it was leading him somewhere. Not to the dwelling beneath the crag, for that was far to the left, but to some sanctuary where he might take shelter with Allifair. But the trail split and was lost in a maze of huge boulders and he found himself up on the bench.

Behind him rose the cliffs, terrace above terrace of shattered porphyry, but already his pursuers were in the cañon below—four Texans and hard-riding Isham. He watched them from the rim as they went whipping down the trail, then settled back and waited grimly. Down the creekbed they galloped, then up and over the point, and down once more into the creek, but, as they saw his horse grazing, they wheeled and took cover, dropping off to reconnoiter on foot. For half an hour or more their heads bobbed up as they crept along the bank of the stream, and then in disgust they strode down to the water and gathered about his horse. He smiled as he saw them cutting circles for sign—they were trying to find his tracks, but he had covered them too well, and, after hunting for several hours, they came back and camped at Cold Spring.

From his look-out among the crags, Hall could hear their loud arguments, and their guesses at where he had gone; he could see their food, almost smell the can of coffee that they boiled over the mesquite coals, but still he lingered, eating acorns to stay his hunger, until at last they mounted and rode on. More than one had shrewdly guessed that he was around there somewhere, but the brush was so thick as to make pursuit hopeless and they were loath to work on foot. So they went away and left him, agreeing to ride the trail first, and Hall began to think about food. On the bench to which he had mounted, the grass stood knee high and there were deer and bear tracks everywhere, but one shot from his rifle would bring the Scarboroughs back, so he prowled through the oaks after turkey. They were there by the hundred, fat gobblers who just escaped him and hens that ran like lightning through the brush, but, as he pursued a brood of young ones, he discovered a nest of eggs and the food question, for the moment, was solved. The eggs were still fresh, and, after eating one raw, he hastened back to his look-out.

Already a feeling of security had come over him, and, as he waited for their return, he worked busily on a turkey trap, which he planned to set at a spring. First he cut some long sticks, to make the top and sides, and then with limber switches he wattled them together, and at evening he took them down to the spring. It lay in the bottom of a brushy gulch and the turkey tracks led down to it everywhere. Cutting out a space above the spring, he planted his wattled cage firmly, and then, digging a trench to lead the turkeys up and under it, he staked off the entrance inside. That was all it was, a fenced trench and a cage, but if any turkey strayed into it and lifted his head, he would try, turkey-like, to find a hole between the slats instead of stooping down to pass out at the hole. Hall concealed the trap with brush and strewed acorns along the trench, and then, as no turkeys came, he built wings leading up to it and hid himself in the oak trees below.

There was a loud gobble from the hillside, the anxious *quilp-quilp* of a hen, and the great birds leaped out and came sailing down through the air to land with a *thump* by the spring. For a moment they crouched frozen as they saw the wings of the trap, but no one had ever hunted them and they soon recovered from their alarm while still others soared down from the heights. An old hen with her little ones came trailing up from the chasm, and Hall watched them with bated breath, but as even these refused to go near his trap, he rose up and made a rush. The hen dodged away, calling loudly to her brood, but in the stampede that followed he drove three of them into the wings and up the trench into the trap. That evening he ate meat, and, when the morning came, he set out to explore his domain.

The chasm up which he had come cut its way through the crags to a level mountain top far beyond, and that, according to Meshackatee, was preëmpted by Old Man Baker, who claimed the whole mountain for himself. Since the Indians had killed his son, no Apache dared venture up there, and Hall made up his mind to follow their example, for Baker had shot every Indian on sight. There was game enough and to spare on the first low bench, and farther up the cañon he discovered a hidden basin, where the deer and wild turkeys swarmed. But what he sought for most was a hiding place among the cliffs, which would shelter him and his mate, and he clambered along the bear track that led off around the point to the first of the dizzy cliff-dwellings.

It proved to be no more than some walls of broken rock, piled up in a shelving hole, and house after house, as he inspected them more closely, turned out to be nothing but skeletons. Most of them had no roofs; they were all hard to get to and entirely too far from water, and the trails that led up to them made it absolutely certain that he would be seen going to and fro. There was only one place that would answer his purpose and it was like an eagle's nest above him. Within a great, arching cave, high up in the cliff, there stood a huge dwelling, with doors and windows sealed and a rampart across its front. It was a medieval castle, transported from dreamland and set like a jewel in the cliff. At the extreme southern side there was a rift in the solid roof that gave promise of a possible descent, but the path that led up to it, if path there ever was, had vanished with the passing of the centuries. Perhaps it had caved off and was buried in the talus that extended along the base of the precipice, but there his castle stood, aloof and unapproachable, whichever way he came.

The days passed, and he became a wild animal, prowling the hillside like a mountain lion as he stalked the young turkeys or sought the hidden way to his castle. He knew it must be there, some cave or hidden passageway, for the rift from above had turned out a mere crack down which a rat could hardly crawl. He sickened of the taste of eggs and broiled turkeys, and of acorns ground up and boiled, yet the sight of that dwelling, high up above the cañon, held him on from day to day. It was a haven of refuge, if he could only reach it—and he knew there must be a path to it somewhere.

From the bench below he often stood and looked up at it, trying to imagine where the path might have passed, and at last he went back and began to explore the chasm, for there could be no other way to the cave. Above, below, and far to the south of the dwelling, the cliff rose, sheer and smooth, but the gateway to the chasm was not so far from the castle that it could not give entrance from the side. Already he had threaded the narrow pathway that led up the bed of the stream, but now he climbed higher and, from the opposite side, looked across for some suggestion of a trail. The cañon wall was steep but not too steep; in places he almost imagined he saw a trail—a row of cat steps here, a stretch of natural stairs, an ascent from shelf to shelf. But of what value was an ascent if it took him to no passageway—what he sought was a way to the cave. He lay idly in the shade, gazing across at the cañon wall, and, as the silence came back, he saw a shadow move down the streambed, pause stealthily, and move again. Then, etched against the granite, a huge mountain lion stood out, tawny red and almost invisible until it moved.

He looked on, still idly, for not since he had come there had he ventured to fire a shot, and the lion, which had been hiding from him, started stealthily up the path that he had been tracing from shelf to shelf. He padded softly up the cat steps, took the stairs at a bound—and disappeared in a high, narrow crack. A half hour later Hall followed in his footsteps, and at the mouth of his cave he received the last assurance that the pathway led to the castle. A cool wind breathed out of it, tainted with the strong musk of lions, and where could it come from but there?

He turned back eagerly to gather pitch pine from a piñon stump, then entered, holding the torch like a club. There was a rustle before him, an uneasy growl, the flash of startled eyes, but still they fled on, and he followed through the darkness until he saw a cleft of light overhead. It merged into an orifice that let in a soft glow and the vision of a skulking form, and then the invisible path, which had held his feet through the darkness, took him out into blinding day. He was standing in the court of his castle in the air and the lion was crouching by the door.

CHAPTER SIXTEEN

Every window and door of the cliff-dwellers' castle had been sealed against man and beast—the mountain lion was at bay, and, as he crouched down to spring, Hall shot him through the head. He leaped into the air and fell, kicking, on his back, and the man took possession of his den. That was the way he had learned of getting what he wanted, and the castle had been his dream. But the doors had been walled up and plastered over with mud a thousand years before and he hesitated to break them in. Perhaps within those walls there lay the bones of chiefs, with their weapons close to their hands, and after the passage of the centuries it seemed an impious thing to break in and disturb their ancient dust. The court alone was large enough to give him room to live and the whole world lay at his feet.

At the crack of his rifle the echoes of Deadman Cañon had awakened from their week-long sleep; they bandied it back and forth, from cliff to distant cliff, the news that a man was there. Hall stood at the rampart and gazed up and down the cañon, and far away to the east, and, as he watched, he saw a horseman drop down into a ravine and ride for the Scarboroughs' stalking ground. The rifle shot had drawn him from a dim trail miles away, so keen had been his ears, and, as he edged out on a point and crept forward to observe the spring, Hall knew he was one of the man-killers. For an hour and more he scouted about the water, but when at last he stepped out into the open, Hall saw at a glance it was Meshackatee.

There was the same huge bulk, the same battered hat, the jumper and the bulging chaps, and the horse that had blended into the landscape like a deer was the buckskin pony, Croppie. Yes, the man was Meshackatee, but what was his mission there, and why did he keep hidden in the brush? A cold hand seemed to take Hall by the throat—perhaps he was hunting for him! Although their relations had been friendly for the short time they were together, since then Meshackatee had had plenty of occasion to regret the trust he had bestowed. Instead of spying upon the Bassetts, Hall had joined them against the Scarboroughs, and later, when Meshackatee had sent him warning by Allifair, he had turned the information against them. Yes, more than that, he had left Meshackatee waiting down the creek while he stayed and did battle with the Slashknives.

Hall watched him from his aerie as he studied the trail for signs, and finally retired to the cliff-dwellings, and then he went back through the cold blackness of the tunnel to store his hiding place with food. What he feared most had happened; the first shot from his gun had brought the manhunters upon him. Perhaps they had been watching through their high-powered glasses, or slipping down to look for his tracks, but now they knew he was there—or at least Meshackatee did—and there was nothing to do but to prepare for a siege. He ran hurriedly to the turkey traps that he had set up the cañon and came back with a pair of big birds, and then he went for acorns and filled his one canteen with water from the ice-cold creek. By that time it was dark and he returned to his look-out to await the next move of his enemies.

All that evening he watched the flicker from Meshackatee's lurking place, the loopholed dwelling above the spring, but the fire was a blind for in the morning Meshackatee came back, leading a pack animal down from the east. During the day he stayed close and Hall put in the time by skinning the mountain lion. But as evening approached again and none of the Scarboroughs rode in, his patience gave way before a yearning for human society, a craving for companionship—and food. So weary had he become of his perpetual turkey diet that he had broiled a steak from the haunch of the panther, and found it far from bad. But he could not live forever without coffee and salt, and, since he must make a move sometime, he decided to make it right then and put Meshackatee's friendship to the test.

As darkness fell, he crept down the gloomy chasm and waded across the creek, and then, with a stealthiness that not even an Indian could excel, he stalked Meshackatee's camp. He had retired within the cliff-dwelling, trusting to the watchfulness of his dog more than to any special vigilance of his own, and, when Hall peered through the doorway, he saw him sitting by the fire, deeply engaged in some mechanical task. In one hand he held a small bow with its string wound around a shaft that seemed to twirl in his grasp like a drill, and in the other he held some object that gleamed in the firelight and looked like a .45 cartridge. The dog, 'Pache, lay asleep on the far side of the fire; there was a whirring noise from the drill, and, when Meshackatee looked up, Hall was standing in the doorway with a questioning look in his eye. If Meshackatee noticed the rifle, held negligently at the hip, he concealed his knowledge well.

"Hello, there!" he hailed, and the dog sprang up barking, his hair bristling forward with rage. "*Aw,* shut up, now, 'Pache!" rebuked Meshackatee indignantly, "you're a hell of a watchdog, I swear! Come in, Hall, come in! Been looking for you everywhere! Shut up, you whelp, or I'll whup ye!"

He reached for a stick and the dog retired, growling, skinning his teeth at the disturber of his dreams.

"Kinder startled him," explained Meshackatee, as Hall stepped inside, but Hall spoke to the point.

"You've been looking for me?" he inquired. "Well, let's come to an understanding . . . are you still in the employ of the Scarboroughs?"

"Hell, no!" burst out Meshackatee with explosive emphasis. "I quit 'em two weeks ago. Their work got too raw for me."

"Then we can be friends," suggested Hall, holding out his hand, and Meshackatee rose up and took it.

"You're whistling," he said, "and I guess mebbe you need one . . . how long since you had a square meal?"

"Well, some time," admitted Hall, "but tell me, first of all, have you heard any news from Allifair?"

"Ye-es," returned Meshackatee, "she's still with the Scarboroughs. I sent an Injun in last week to look around. He said there was lots of cowboys, and two womenfolk cooking, and the cowboys was rounding up stock. But I heard from other sources that Miz Zoolah has written home and told Allifair's brothers to come out."

"What . . . to get her?"

"Or you," hinted Meshackatee grimly, and Hall nodded his head regretfully.

"I was afraid of that," he admitted. "Cal and Ewing are hard men . . . we've had several encounters already."

"Well, the word I git is that the Scarboroughs are sending everywhere to hire all the gunmen they can. And, since they've killed Sharps and old Henry Bassett, they've come right out into the open. Everybody always knew they had a weakness for stray stock, but now they've joined a gang that works in three states and steals horses from plumb down in Texas. That judge down in Tonto that give the Maverick Basin boys a tip to settle their differences with a Winchester . . . well, he claims he never said it, but he sure played merry hell, because the wrong outfit is coming out on top. Them ranchers down on the Verde and clean to Geronimo are making an awful howl, and this gang of Texas horse thieves is driving their stock off by the hundreds and running them up into the basin. It's a regular hold-out, a horse-thieves' exchange, where Arizona horses are traded into Texas and Texas bronc's swapped the other way. I been down in Tonto and the folks is all het up over it . . . some talk of a vigilance committee, and so forth."

He paused, and, as Hall stared moodily into the fire, Meshackatee reached over and picked up a coffee pot.

"I'll cook you a little grub," he volunteered briskly, and Hall came back from his dreams. "Of course," went on Meshackatee, having won his attention, "this business don't mean much to you. All you want is your girl and. . . ."

"Yes, but how am I to get her?" demanded Hall fiercely.

"Well . . . ," began Meshackatee, and then he stopped. "Of course there's always a way."

"How do you mean?" inquired Hall, as he failed to elucidate, but Meshackatee only mumbled in his beard.

"Drink some coffee," he said, "and git some grub under your belt. A man is a mouse when he's starved."

He heated up some bread and a kettle of beans, and cut a can of fruit, and, when Hall had eaten, Meshackatee took up the discussion exactly where he had let it drop.

"There's always a way"—he nodded impressively—"provided you've got the nerve. Them Texans are proddy, I'll admit that from the start, and Isham has turned plumb bad. Always thought he was a blow-hard, a big bag of wind, but the scoundrel has turned out a killer. I'm nothing but a gunman, or that's what they call me, and I can't say I'm squeamish a bit. When them sheepmen come in, I was in the forefront of the battle . . . might have killed one or two of 'em myself. And furthermore, when they hired Paine and them Slashknife boys to ride in and clean up on the Bassetts, I could stand for that stuff, too. It was rough, but they had a fighting chance. But this downright murdering, like shooting old Henry and leaving

Sharps out for the hogs . . . well, right there was where I quit.
But I didn't quit quick enough. That Isham had gone bad, and
he damned nigh got my scalp." He rumpled his hair thought-
fully and shook his head at the fire. "You never can tell," he
added.

"Did he attempt to kill you?" asked Hall, but Meshackatee
shrugged it away.

"Never mind," he grumbled. "That's between him and me.
But lemme give you a tip. If you meet up with Isham, you go
for your gun right away. But you won't meet nobody . . . that
ain't the way they fight. The first thing you meet will be a Forty-
Five explosive bullet . . . they're fighting from cover entirely.
I've been down to Tonto talking with the sheriff of the county
and a few other old *compadres* of mine, and it's the consensus of
opinion that Maverick Basin is going to be damned unhealthy.
Especially for officers and such. At the same time, as I said,
there's always a way. . . ."

"Well, what is that way?" broke in Hall impatiently. "Are you
thinking of going back?"

"I might be," admitted Meshackatee, "but I heard a gun down
here yesterday, and I thought mebbe it might be Isham. He's
the *hombre* I'm gunning for, to tell you the truth, and so I've
been watching the trail. And in the meantime, while my time
was idle on my hands, I've been fixing up some more of these."

He picked up one of the cartridges upon which he had been
working and Hall examined it critically. A hole had been bored
into the heart of the lead bullet and a smaller cartridge neatly
imbedded.

"One of them explosive bullets," boasted Meshackatee
shamelessly. "I claim to have invented 'em, myself. A Twenty-
Two blank, set exactly in the middle of it, and the minute she
hits something . . . *zingo!* . . . she blows up like a bomb. Maybe
you saw how they worked when we were chousing them sheep?

Well, the Scarboroughs are shooting them at men."

"I know that." Hall nodded. "But you spoke of some plan."

"Oh, sure," replied Meshackatee, "well, what I had in mind was to go back and try these on them."

"And then?"

"Well, take to the brush, out-Injun 'em if we can . . . I'll admit it's kinder risky."

"I see," murmured Hall, and fell silent again while Meshackatee watched him narrowly.

"Of course," went on Meshackatee, "there's a whole bunch of them Texans."

"That doesn't worry me a bit," put in Hall abruptly. "I've been doing this kind of fighting all my life. But I promised Miss Randolph I'd keep out of this trouble and I aim to make my word good. At the same time, if the Scarboroughs have sent for her brothers. . . ."

"They sure have," affirmed Meshackatee, "and I'll tell you how I know it. One of them neutrals came out to bring 'em some cartridges and he showed me the letter himself. It was addressed to Cal Randolph, somewhere back in Kentucky. . . ."

"That's all right," interrupted Hall, "I believe you. It's only a question of whether I can get her away before her brothers arrive. Because, of course, you must see that I'm sure to lose her if I shoot Cal or Ewing now. I've simply got to disappear the moment they arrive and stay hidden until they go home."

"Well, we can fix it to git her," spoke up Meshackatee at length, "or at least we can make a try. But the first thing to do is to bushwhack old Isham and put the fear of God in their hearts. They're riding the hills in bands, or so they tell me, out gunning for Winchester and young Bill, and there's a bunch of them Bassett neutrals that'll soon have to move if someone don't tap off Isham. But here's one *hombre*, I'm telling you, that ain't skeered of them all . . . if I can jest git one man for a pardner. A man has got to sleep, and that's where they ketch you, unless you happen to have a pardner to keep watch."

"That's true," agreed Hall, "and I'd be more than pleased to join you if it were not for my promise to Allifair. But under the circumstances, Meshackatee. . . . ."

"What, do you mean to say," burst out Meshackatee provocatively, "that you're going to let Isham git away with it? Didn't he try to shoot you down the same time he killed Sharps, and leave you lay for the hogs? Didn't he shoot at your girl when she run out to save you and all but kill her, too? I was under the impression. . . . ."

"Just a moment," broke in Hall, looking him straight in the eye, "I believe in telling the truth. Back in Kentucky, where I come from, a man who would attack a woman would be run out of the country over night . . . and his own family would do their part . . . but I have promised my intended not to join in on this feud, unless by so doing I can save her. But before we go any further . . . why is it, my friend, that you are so keen for this desperate adventure? As I said before, I believe in telling the truth."

"Well, there then!" exclaimed Meshackatee, throwing back his shirt and revealing a small star underneath. "I'm a deputy sheriff, that's why. The sheriff and all his deputies was afraid to come in here . . . leastwise they wouldn't none of 'em come . . . and I told 'em, gimme a badge and ten dollars a day, and I'd go in and git him myself. Yes, Isham . . . he's the man . . . and I figger on shooting him on sight. When I quit and called for my pay, he told me to go to hell or he'd fill me full of lead, and then, by grab, he made his brag before them Texans that he'd helped do this job on my ears. Well, if he did, he's the very identical rascal I'm looking for, and it's him or me, that's all. Now, the cards are on the table and you can join in or pull out . . . if you stick, you're a deputy sheriff."

114

"I'll stick," flashed back Hall, and Meshackatee grabbed his hand. "I knowed it!" he said, and laughed.

CHAPTER SEVENTEEN

It was a failing of Hall's, this instant response to the call of any friend for aid, and yet, when Meshackatee laid his plans before him, he was glad he had agreed to join him. For Meshackatee above all things was a man of action, and action, with Hall, was a necessity. All the days he had spent prowling in the hills like an animal had been wasted, as he looked back at them now, for Allifair's brothers would come, and come soon, if only to kill a McIvor. They were hard men to deal with, or had proved so to him, and there was many an old score that might be settled even yet if they could pick up his trail again. He had been lost before, given up for dead by his parents and the men of both clans, but this call from their aunt, and their sister's love affair, would bring them from wherever they lurked. And now, unless he was willing to see her snatched away, he must strike a last blow to win Allifair.

"No, I'll tell you," expounded Meshackatee, "they's no use doing anything until we've throwed the hooks into Isham. He's the leader of the gang, and, as long as he's there, you can't git away with that girl. He's got men on the trails, and Injun spies out everywhere, to say nothing of them organized horse thieves, and, whichever way you ride, he's going to reach out and git you . . . unless, of course, you git him. Now here's the proposition, and I'll put it to you straight, jest exactly as it was put up to me. We're deputy sheriffs, see, drawing ten dollars *per diem* to serve these here warrants on the Scarboroughs, but I've been told unofficially that the county'll be jest as well pleased if they're killed while resisting arrest. The idee is to git 'em to resist. Tonto County, as I understand it, has got jest enough money to pay for deputies, but none for expensive court proceedings. When it comes to a showdown, the Scarborough outfit has got more money than the county . . . and you know what these lawyers are like. But that ain't our business, we're here to serve these warrants, and I'm going to start in on Isham.

"Now there's a man, Hall, that I thought I knowed well, and I always claimed he was a coward. It jest shows how you sometimes git fooled. When it comes to a showdown, that jasper always weakened, but it was jest because he was foxy. He knowed if he drawed the other feller would git him, and so he never drawed. He hired gunmen to do his fighting because gunmen was cheap and he wanted to keep out of jail, but when them Slashknife boys fell down, he seen right there he'd have to do his dirty work himself. That was the time when the dog hair cropped out on him and I seen, by grab, he was a killer. Not a gunfighter, mind ye . . . and they're dangerous enough . . . but one of these sneaking, calculating kind. He fights like the Apaches, never showing a head and always shooting from ambush, and the only way we'll git him is to go him one better . . . we've got to out-Injun him, that's all."

"I'm ready," replied Hall. "Why not start right now?" And Meshackatee took him at his word.

They headed off east up the dim Indian trail that Meshacka-tee had followed down to water. As the stars wheeled in their courses, Hall saw their direction change until at last they were going northwest. They had scrambled up a wash, and then on up grassy slopes that led to the big ridge behind, and from there they had turned north, following a trail that dipped and twisted as it skirted the east slope of Turkey Creek. They rode and walked by turns, driving the pack animal before them. As the east began to flush, they took to high ground and camped through the long, sultry day.

The summer heat was at its height, the close, oppressive heat that presages torrential rains to come, and from the top of their butte they could see the white thunderheads, riding majestically up above the Mogollon Rim. Below them lay the cañon with Turkey Creek at its bottom, and, still farther northwest, the broad swales of Maverick Basin showed dimly through a pass in the hills. Hall looked it all over through Meshackatee's big glasses, when it came his turn to stand guard, and then he looked back along the trail they had followed, trying to fix every landmark in his mind. For if all went well, the time would soon come when he would be fleeing through the night with Allifair, and every butte and ridge, every turn in that dim trail, must be stamped indelibly on his memory. He traced it out again, noting each landmark through his glasses, and then suddenly he picked up an Indian. He had stepped out from some scrub oaks and was examining their tracks, where they had passed through a sandy swale, and, as he disappeared into the brush, Hall ran and wakened Meshackatee, but the Apache did not show himself again.

"He's down in some gulch," observed Meshackatee sagely, "probably legging it to take the news to Isham. Two white men, one on foot, and two horses, one drove ahead, and a dog . . . well, that will be Meshackatee. And the man on foot . . . the chances are good that Isham will guess it's you. Well, watch along Turkey Creek, and if you see anyone crossing, wake me up and we'll make a quick move."

Hall watched, and, as the day wore on toward evening, he saw what Meshackatee had feared. Six horsemen in single file came trotting down the creek, half hidden behind the tall brush, but when Meshackatee came, the enemy had vanished again and the trails were bare—too bare.

"We'll move," stated Meshackatee, "as soon as it's dark, and, if you're game, I am . . . we'll ride across country and try to come out at the Rock House. Might as well head for the place we're going to, even if I don't know the way none too well."

"All right," agreed Hall, "and, if we find cover in time, I'll slip down and spy on the house."

"Bad business," grumbled Meshackatee, "don't like this a little bit. Them cowboys are out for our hair."

They remained at the look-out until it was dark and then, packing swiftly, struck out to the west, following cow trails clear to the creek. There they watered their horses and started up the other side, but the cañon that they ascended boxed up near the summit and they had to return to the creek. Meshackatee's plans had gone awry, putting him in a very bad humor, but, after thinking it over, he moved up a side cañon and took shelter on a bench above the stream.

Here they tied the horses in a narrow cove that was surrounded on three sides by wooded slopes, and then, with his dog stretched out against his back, Meshackatee sprawled and went to sleep. But the failure of their plans had left Hall uneasy—he did not approve of this camp above the trail. As morning approached, he rose up silently and felt his way down to the stream. This was the hour that he dreaded, just before the break of day, and he crept along the ground regardless of the dew that weighed down the heavy grass.

There had been noises in the night and 'Pache had growled repeatedly; some wild cattle had jumped suddenly and fled. As he drew near the water, he noticed that the grass had been trampled on the opposite side of the stream. He slipped down closer, hardly stirring a twig as he moved, and the first flush of dawn showed men's tracks in the sand—and the dew had been knocked from the grass. He lay silently, his heart thumping; there was a stir across the creek, a stir and the movement of a head. That was enough—he glided away like a rattlesnake, and Meshackatee woke up with a jump. They were surrounded—he knew that from the look in Hall's eyes—and, catching up his gun from the fold of his blanket, he rolled over behind a big rock.

"Where are they at?" he whispered, and, when Hall told him, he grunted and began to pile up rocks. Hall dug in, also, making a loophole through which to shoot and laid out his cartridges in rows. 'Pache, sensing the enemy, crouched down anxiously between them, growling low and sniffing the wind. A death-like silence fell upon the narrow cañon as they settled back to wait for the attack, but not a bush stirred—the Scarboroughs were still hoping they would saddle up and ride down the hill. Ride up to their very guns and then with one volley they could snuff out their lives together. But their ambush had been detected and now Meshackatee and Hall were searching the brushy hillside for a target.

"No use," complained Meshackatee, "they must've heard us digging. Let's start something, before they scatter out."

He took off his old hat and stuck it on a stick, and, as it bobbed above the boulder, an explosive bullet struck it, spattering the ground about them with lead. 'Pache yelped as débris struck him and cringed down beside Meshackatee who was cursing at the hole in his hat. Then Hall saw a movement below the smoke puff and answered with a shot that drew a volley. The whole hillside seemed to belch forth smoke, but the bullets for the most part went high; the Scarboroughs were below them, hidden away among the boulders that had fallen from the rimrock above.

"They can't reach us." Meshackatee chuckled, snuggling up to his loophole and shooting back at the smoke, but a crash from behind brought them both to a right-about and raised a cheer from below. The explosive bullets had stampeded their pack horse and they were just in time to see him go smashing through the brush toward the creekbed below.

"Makes no difference," grumbled Meshackatee, "don't need him now, nohow . . . be lucky to git out of here afoot."

Hall made no comment but down in his heart he agreed with Meshackatee fully—they would be lucky to get out alive. Behind them the steep slopes were sparsely covered with timber, but not enough to protect them in their flight, and the sound of the firing would bring the whole Scarborough clan to make their position worse. It was a dangerous place to be, and yet no more dangerous than others where he had been compelled to make a stand. And he had often observed that, where both sides were shooting from cover, it was seldom that anyone was hurt. Only one thing was necessary—they must maintain their position until darkness should cover up their flight. He peeped out through his loophole, shooting warily at stray smoke puffs, and they settled themselves for the siege.

But the men that they were fighting were not satisfied to wait; they had other strings to their bow. As Hall and Meshackatee lay behind their rock shelter, a bullet struck between them.

"Judas Priest!" exclaimed Meshackatee, as his dog ran off yelping, and then, seeing the smoke from a point across the creek, he hastily changed his position. Hall piled up rocks before them, but Meshackatee lay watching, and, when the next bullet came, he shot.

"Behind that big boulder," he said. "You watch me smoke him out of that."

"Haven't got time," answered Hall, but Meshackatee did not smile—he was slipping an explosive cartridge into his gun. He thrust out his rifle and lay, sighting along the barrel, and at a puff from the boulder he fired. Another bullet struck their rock pile, dangerously near, but the man behind the boulder leaped up as if he were shot, and Hall saw that it was an Indian. He

121

darted off along the hillside with Meshackatee still shooting at him, and at the second shot he fell. But even when he was down, Meshackatee shot him again, and the Indian lay a huddle in the sun.

"I'll show you," muttered Meshackatee, "you dog-goned rat-eater. You're the *hombre* that's been raising all this hell. Well, see how you like that, and mebbe the rest of them Apaches will learn to lay off of Meshackatee."

He turned to Hall and nodded triumphantly.

"What'd I tell ye?" he said. "Did you see me smoke him out? Busted a big explosive bullet on that rock jest behind him and burned him up with hot lead. But I knowed, by grab, no *Tejano* could bushwhack me . . . they've gone and hired Apaches."

"There's another one!" exclaimed Hall, as another plunging shot came over the top of their fort, and Meshackatee grabbed for his cartridges.

"Better git out of here," he said, and was turning to scuttle away when a rifle opened up down the creek. It was shooting fast and almost rhythmically, and another lighter gun joined in, then there was a tattoo of answering shots, trailing off into silence as the fighters emptied their magazines.

"What's that?" asked Hall, and Meshackatee shook his head—he was watching the rocky hill. Something moved among the boulders, his rifle roared out again, and, as a tall Texan broke to run, they both opened fire. He dropped his gun and ran on.

"They're all going!" exclaimed Hall, turning to shoot toward the creekbed, and now there was no answer as with harrying shots they followed the flight of the bushwhackers. Whoever they were, they were fleeing in a panic—the battle had been won, but by whom?

CHAPTER EIGHTEEN

They waited, these two men who had dared invade the Scarborough stronghold and, daring it, had almost paid the price, then Meshackatee raised a hail.

"Wa-a-hooo!" he called, and, as his big voice woke the echoes, there was an answering yell from below. A man, invisible as a spotted fawn when it walks in the shadow of leaves, came rustling up the cañon, and at last he spoke from the hill.

"Wahoo yourself," he challenged. "Who the hell are you fellers, anyway?"

"I'm Meshackatee," returned that gentleman, "and here's Hall. . . ."

"Oh, Hall, eh?" spoke up the voice. "This is Winchester Bassett. Come down, boys, and I'll stake you to a horse."

They crept down through the shadows and met him at the creek, still smiling but without his jaunty air. A thick growth of black beard made his face look deathly pale, his clothes were hanging in shreds, and, as he wrung Hall's hand, he had a wild look in his eyes although he tried to conceal it with a smile.

"Well, well, Hall," he said, "I'm sure glad to see you. And you, too, Meshackatee . . . how are you? But, say, we'd better go, because the Scarboroughs will be back and we don't want to git caught in this brush. Heard you shooting down here, and Bill and me took a chance . . . we winged two of 'em and captured all their horses."

"I knowed it!" exclaimed Meshackatee. "I almost knowed

that it was you. They ain't many men, I'll say, that can work a Winchester that fast. . . ."

"I was named after it." Winchester grinned. "How're you fixed for ammunition?"

"Whole pack load!" answered Meshackatee. "Thought you boys might be short. Come on, let's go bring it down."

They caught up their frightened horses and threw packs on the skittish pack animal. Winchester had gone back to join Bill, and, when they arrived, they found the Bassetts in a rock pile for so much bushwhacking had got on their nerves.

"Help yourselves, boys," invited Winchester, waving his hand at the Scarborough horses, which were tied among the willows by the creek, "and for cripes' sake make it brief."

They mounted helter-skelter, driving the spare horses before them as they dashed across the creek and away, but, when they had put a mile between themselves and the treacherous hillside, Winchester held up his hand for a halt.

"No rush now, fellers," he said. "We'll jest see what happens. And by the way, what's the chances for a smoke?"

"Good"—Meshackatee beamed—"got lots of tobaccy. I knowed you boys would be short."

"Oh, you did, eh?" observed Winchester as he took the makings to roll a quick smoke, and he cocked his head at Bill.

"Yep, brought lo-ots of tobaccy," repeated Meshackatee hospitably, as he began to unlash his pack. "I'll git you them cartridges now."

"Damned good of you," murmured Winchester, "but what's the big idea? I ain't curious. I jest want to know."

"Oh, didn't I tell ye?" Meshackatee grinned. "Me and Hall are deputy sheriffs."

"The hell!" scoffed Winchester, and Bill stopped smoking long enough to feel for his gun.

"That's a fact," returned Meshackatee. "Got warrants for the

Scarboroughs. Want you and Bill to help serve 'em."

There was a silence then as Winchester tugged at his mustache and considered the possibilities of the case.

"Well, I'll tell you, Meshackatee," he said at last, "of course it's all right, but, after what's happened, Bill and I don't want 'em arrested. We want to see 'em killed."

"No more'n natural," conceded Meshackatee, "but you understand there's such a thing as the law. I can't shut my eyes to no such violations, but . . . well, my orders, boys, is dead or alive. I reckon you understand."

"*Uhr* . . . that's different," replied Winchester, as Meshackatee winked at him, but Bill was still in the dark.

"Yes, law," he burst out, "a man get lots of protection from you deputy sheriffs and such. Here them Scarboroughs have been chasing us like a couple of wild animals for well nigh onto a month. . . ."

"Never mind, Bill." Winchester smiled. "Don't you git the idee? We serve these here warrants with a six-shooter."

"The Scarboroughs," put in Meshackatee, "is charged with first-degree murder, for killing your father and Sharps."

"Oh." Bill nodded, and for a moment sat in gloomy silence. "Well, gimme a star, then," he added.

They rode on along the ridge, keeping well up above Turkey Creek and watching for the Scarboroughs below. As no horsemen appeared, they finally skirted the whole valley and came out in the hills above the basin. The ground here was open, with waving slopes of grass and timber along the summits, and they made a camp among the oak trees, while they staked out their horses and swept the plain with their field glasses. They had a pair apiece now, for the men who had ambushed them had left all their glasses on their saddles. As Meshackatee surveyed the spoils, he chuckled in his beard, for the day had not promised so well.

"Pretty slick, boys," he said. "Two horses apiece now, and these field glasses are sure good for weak eyes. I feel it in my bones I'll soon have a big posse . . . say, ain't that one of the Scarboroughs by the house?"

"It's Red," responded Hall, "and he's riding my horse. I'd know that little roan anywhere."

"Remember that time when he tried to trade you out of him? Well, that's Red . . . he's crazy about horses."

"Yes, and I'm crazy, too," said Hall, still watching him through his glasses. "I'll bet you I get that horse back."

"How?" demanded Meshackatee, but Hall shrugged his shoulders.

"How does anybody get back a horse?" he asked.

"By cracky," burst out Meshackatee, "that gives me an idee! Do you mean you're going to steal 'im? Well, we'll pull a little Injun stuff, jest to pay 'em for this morning, and I bet you we come pretty nigh gitting Red."

"Well, count me in on that," put in Winchester quietly. "It was Red that shot the old man."

"I know this is good," said Meshackatee, "because I saw it pulled off once myself. The Apaches danged near worked it on me. Instead of stealing that horse, jest slip up and pull his picket pin, and like any horse he'll make for the hills. It ain't natural for a horse to stay out on them flats. They always like to git up on high ground. Well, let 'im ramble till daylight, and then see where he's gone to . . . and be there when Red comes up."

"Let me do it," clamored Bill, but Winchester brushed him aside.

"I'm the oldest," he said. "I claim Red."

"I'll release that horse myself," stated Hall. "If Red follows it, that's nothing to me."

"Winchester's surest," decided Meshackatee. "But whoever takes this job has got to do it my way."

"All right," agreed Winchester, his eyes suddenly gleaming. "Go ahead. What you want me to do?"

"I want you to rise up," said Meshackatee solemnly, "and say . . . 'Surrender, in the name of the law!' "

"He'll take that to hell with 'im," predicted Winchester grimly. "I wish I could say it to Isham."

"That's my job," replied Meshackatee. "I claim Isham."

"You can have him," conceded Winchester, "if I don't git him first. But what's your grievance against Isham?"

"Never mind," returned Meshackatee, "but I'm telling you right now . . . I claim Isham Scarborough myself. That's what brought me back to these parts."

"Well, we won't quarrel." Winchester smiled, and, going off by himself, he began to pace up and down. "Come on," he said at last, "they can probably see us through field glasses. Let's saddle up and start off north. We can come back after it's dark."

"Good idee," agreed Meshackatee, "but ain't they a cowardly lot of gun-toters . . . afraid to come out and fight the four of us?"

"That ain't the way they work it," said Winchester. "We'll give 'em a dose of their own medicine. But honest, boys, I can't hardly wait to git my gun on Red Scarborough."

They rode off slowly, keeping a scout before and behind to protect them from possible surprise, and, when it was dark, they made their way across Turkey Creek, taking shelter in the hills behind the store. From their hiding place on the heights, they could see the lights down at the Rock House, and lanterns bobbing to and fro. Shortly after midnight, armed only with his pistols, Hall McIvor set off on his quest. He walked warily from the first, for the ambush of that morning had taught him to fear the Apaches, but if they were skulking nearby, he passed by them unobserved and crept close to the silent Rock House.

For an hour he lay watching it, half tempted to climb the Indian mound and steal a secret interview with Allifair, but the hounds were restless and noisy and the time had not come for him to jeopardize her safety again. The Scarboroughs ruled the basin with the power of feudal barons, their retainers were on every trail, and until their pride was broken, until they, too, had learned to fear, it was useless to oppose their will. He crept closer through the damp grass to where his high-headed roan, Blue, was nervously circling his stake, and, creeping up silently, he worked the picket pin loose and watched Blue as he walked away. At first Blue started south, heading back toward his home, but, as the hounds rushed out barking, he turned and circled west, still dragging the rope and pin.

At the first peep of dawn, they located Blue with their glasses, standing stiffly at the foot of a hill. As the sun rose and touched him, Blue woke from his trance-like sleep and moved up toward a point. There, following his horse nature, he intended to stand, basking in the sun until the chill was out of his limbs, after which he would fall to feeding, enjoying his freedom to the full before his new master should trail him from the plain. In hiding not a hundred yards away there was a man, waiting patiently with his rifle in his hands. When Blue raised his head and looked back toward the Rock House, Winchester could see a lone man riding out. It was Red, mounted bareback on a horse he had picked up, following rapidly along the broad trail. As he spied his missing mount, he cut straight across the valley, coming up the grassy swale at a lope. Winchester crouched down behind a bush and breathed on his hands—his hour of vengeance had come.

Red rode up toward the horse, unconscious of any danger until a man rose just below him, a man with a rifle in his hands.

"Surrender," he said, "in the name of the law!" But Red sat staring, open-mouthed. Then he whirled his horse and Winchester shot him twice, leaving him dead where he pitched to the ground.

"Here's your horse," he said, as he rode back to camp, and Hall took the trembling Blue in silence.

"Good enough!" pronounced Meshackatee, and they started off north, for the Scarboroughs were beginning to swarm.

CHAPTER NINETEEN

There cannot be a war without violence and bloodshed, nor can all the losses be on one side. No matter which side is right, or which has the strongest battalions, death holds a level hand. The Scarboroughs had killed Sharps and old Henry Bassett, but now the scales had turned and Red, their finest rifle shot, had been shot down by Winchester Bassett. A posse of four men had ridden into their stronghold and held fast to Indian tactics. Death had risen up and snatched away Red. Yet even with the body of their brother before them, the Scarboroughs declined to fight in the open.

No swarm of vengeful Texans came spurring on their trail as Meshackatee led the way north, riding boldly up the trail that led like a highway toward the Mogollon Rim. At the divide above Cañon Creek they stopped. Here, although they were hidden in the pines, they could watch the trail both ways, and it was time to cook coffee and rest. And if, as might happen, any Scarborough men passed by, they could give them tit for tat. For a month and more the Scarboroughs in their arrogance had held up every wayfarer on this trail, and, if a man did not belong to their secret organization, he was destined to proceed on foot. When, late in the afternoon, they spied a horse herd coming south, they fairly romped to cover.

The horses, which were jaded from their long drive over the rocks, came toiling up the zigzag trail, and the posse let them pass, but as the two Texans who were driving them came up with the drag, they sensed mischief and dashed back down the hill. Lead slugs and explosive bullets struck the ground all about them, and, as they forded the creek, the Bassetts took after them while the others rounded up the horses.

"Them's Mormon horses," declared Meshackatee after they had stopped them on a flat. "I know about half of them brands. We'll jest hold 'em a while and see who shows up . . . may git some of these Texicans yet."

They went to their look-out, leaving the horses to graze, and almost immediately Bill and Winchester appeared, riding low and spurring like mad.

"Injuns!" they yelled as they scrambled up the point and dropped down behind the rocks. "Apaches, as sure as hell!"

"Where at?" demanded Meshackatee. "Them Apaches ain't on the warpath, and hain't been since the Apache Kid."

"Well, all right," panted Bill, "but I'll bet ye we seen twenty. And when we run across 'em, they chased us."

"There they are!" said Winchester, pointing to a string of half-naked horsemen, "and if them ain't Apaches, I'm a liar."

"Leave 'em to me," bragged Meshackatee, "because that's where I shine. We'll try 'em with a little sign talk."

He stepped out on the point where he could be seen plainly from below and raised his right hand in the peace sign.

"Wahoo!" he bellowed. "Wahoo Meshackatee!" But the Indians only circled and stared at him. They were savage-looking creatures, with their long black hair bound back out of their eyes with red handkerchiefs, but after a second look Meshackatee ripped out an oath and came striding back to the posse.

"*Aw*, hell," he exclaimed, "them ain't no Injuns! It's nothing but a passel of white men."

"How do you know?" demanded Bill. "Jest because they don't savvy your sign language. . . ."

"*Aw*, cripes, I know an Injun!" burst out Meshackatee

indignantly. "I can tell 'em by the way they set a horse. We'll try 'em with a little U.S.A."

He stepped out on the point and hailed them again, and a man rode out from the rest. He was mounted on a mule, and the minute he saw him, Hall knew it was Grimes. It was not the mule alone; it was the thrust of his head and the handy way he carried his rifle.

"Hello there!" shouted Hall, stepping out on a rock, and Grimes stopped his mule and looked up.

"Don't know you," he announced, "but damn your black hearts, we've come to git back our horses!"

"That's Grimes, the sheepman," explained Hall over his shoulder, and Meshackatee stepped down behind a rock.

"You talk to him," he grumbled. "I got no use for a sheep-man." And Winchester and Bill nodded assent.

"Yes, sure it's Grimes," yelled the pseudo-Indian, "but who in damnation are you?"

"My name is Hall," he answered shortly. "I met you down at the Bassetts' "

"Oh, that preacher guy," observed the sheepman sarcastically. "Well, what are you doing up here?"

"I'm a deputy sheriff," retorted Hall. "What does your business happen to be?"

"A deputy sheriff!" whooped Grimes. "Hey, boys, here's a deputy sheriff!"

He laughed and the gang of make-believe Apaches came riding up to join him.

"Seems to amuse them," remarked Hall, and Meshackatee muttered an oath while the Bassetts looked on in grim silence.

"Bunch of Mormons," growled Winchester, "rigged out with horse tails and handkerchiefs . . . kinder reminds me of the Mountain Meadow Massacre."

"All the same," spoke up Meshackatee, "we might use the

danged jaspers. Git 'em to go down and clean up on the Scarboroughs."

"Why not?" chimed in Hall. "This is no time for petty differences. Shall I tell them we'll give back their horses?"

"Sure," replied Meshackatee, "but they've got to prove ownership. Otherwise they'll claim the whole band. Go down and see what you can do."

Hall swung up on his horse and rode down the trail, and, as he came up to the Mormons, they reined to one side, leaving Grimes to do the talking.

"Howdy do, Hall?" he began. "Do you know anything about our horses? So you're a deputy sheriff, hey?"

"Yes, I'm a deputy sheriff," answered Hall evenly, "and I can't see that it's in any way a joke. There are three more officers up there in the rocks, and I'd advise you to show a little more respect."

"Oh, certainly," mocked Grimes, "you're jest the *hombres* we're looking for. A big gang of horse thieves has been raiding our ranches and driving off our stock for a month. Not gitting any protection, we have organized to run 'em down and hang every scoundrel we can ketch, but now, of course, all we have to do is to report our losses to you."

"Yes, that's right," said Hall, "just give me a list of the animals, so there won't be any mistake."

"Any mistake!" repeated Grimes. "Well, by grab, it seems to me you look more like a horse thief than we do. How's the Scarborough boys gitting along these days? I believe you was staying with the Bassetts?"

"Yes, I was staying with the Bassetts," replied Hall. "Anything more you'd like to know?"

"I asked you," sneered Grimes, who seemed determined to pick a quarrel, "how your friends, the Scarboroughs, are gitting along."

"Why, not so well," returned Hall. "Red was killed only this morning. It was a case of resisting arrest."

"Killed!" cried Grimes, and then he spurred forward and held out a hairy hand. "By hooky," he exclaimed, "I sure apologize, Mister Hall, for any little thing I may have said. I'm sure glad to meet you, and my friends and neighbors here will be proud to shake your hand."

He introduced the Mormon ranchmen, most of whom had laid off their disguises, and then returned to the matter at hand.

"Are you in charge of this posse?" he asked. "Because we'd like to find out about them horses."

"No, I'm not," replied Hall. "Meshackatee is in command, and the other two deputies are Bassetts. You remember them . . . Winchester and Bill?"

"You don't say!" exclaimed Grimes, leaning over in his saddle. "Is that the way the ground lays? Because if that's the case, I can git you a bunch of deputies that will serve without money and without price. All we ask is a whack at the Scarboroughs."

"We can talk that over later," responded Hall, "but I'm sure we'd be glad to have you. Now about those horses . . . we just captured a big band that a couple of young Texans were driving."

"Good," chorused the Mormons, suddenly starting up the trail, but Hall motioned them back.

"And my orders," he went on, "were that each man should describe his animals in order to avoid mistakes."

"Give 'im his way, boys, give 'im his way!" spoke up Grimes with assumed heartiness. "He's an officer of the law, after all. And right now, Mister Hall, I want to offer my services to arrest the last Scarborough for horse stealing."

Hall nodded obliviously, for all the Mormons in unison were calling off a list of their horses, and after they had written the brands and colors on chance papers, he led the way to the herd. Meshackatee and the Bassetts rode along to deliver the animals, but when the lists had been filled, there was a general clamor for other horses, which the ranchers claimed as their own. At first Meshackatee resisted them, demanding receipts for the animals, but, as they became more insistent, he threw up his hands and told them to take the whole herd.

"And git the hell out of here," he added under his breath—which the Mormons proceeded to do.

It was late in the evening, but, rushing the herd before them, they started back up the trail at a gallop. Only Grimes, the sheepman, stayed, and he stemmed every rebuff until Meshackatee made him a deputy.

CHAPTER TWENTY

A common cause will bring strange people together, but a common hatred will make them like brothers. The Bassetts suspected Grimes of fishing for sheep rights, and he knew they had run out on him in his fight, and a month before Meshackatee had been a gunman, engaged in fighting all three of them, but a common desire to get revenge on the Scarboroughs made them partners, if not exactly friends. And Hall, who would have quit all four of them in a minute if there was any other way of winning Allifair, plunged heart and soul into the council of war that was to plan the downfall of Isham. For it was Isham after all who was the head and front of the Scarboroughs, and he had a genius for making men hate him.

"I'm for riding up to his house," declared Grimes, swaying truculently where he sat, "and shooting it out, right there. We could slip up on 'em after dark."

"Nope, that house is a fort," vetoed Meshackatee instantly. "He could pot the whole bunch of us through them loopholes. And that passel of hounds would raise such a hooraw you couldn't git nigh the place."

"And besides," interposed Hall, "there are the womenfolk to think of. . . ."

"They didn't think of ours," broke in Bill resentfully. "And for all we know, Maw's dead. They went up to the store and told Johnson they'd kill him if he sold the old lady anything."

"Well, let's begin right there," suggested Hall pacifically.

"Let's go down to that store and hold up the storekeeper and take Missus Bassett some supplies. I'm ready to start right now."

"Nope, not tonight," objected Meshackatee cannily. "They're liable to be out somewhere looking for us."

"Well, I'll tell you," suggested Winchester, "let's go after them two horse thieves that Bill and I were chasing. They headed right up that side cañon."

"That's the talk!" agreed Grimes, springing eagerly to his feet. "Them's the boys we want to git. D'ye think you can follow their trail?"

"They's a cabin up there," explained Winchester, "kind of a hold-out for horse thieves, I reckon. The chances are good they'll come back to it."

"Well, let's wait till before daylight," suggested the practical Meshackatee, "and ketch 'em jest at dawn."

"It's a dirty damned way of fighting," grumbled Winchester morosely, "but I'm game . . . they pulled it on me."

So they slept until the morning star, glowing round like a ball, gave warning that daylight was near. Then, with Winchester ahead, they forded the roaring creek and followed a beaten trail up the cañon. Not one or two horses had trampled that broad path—a band had been over it, and more than one band—and they could see the Texans' tracks leading on. At dawn they sighted a house, a small, chunky cabin built from the biggest logs that could be moved and chock against it was a corral where two jaded ponies stood drooping inside the bars. It stood in a little opening, tucked up under the north hill, and they withdrew to lay their plans.

"We'll surround it," directed Meshackatee, "two men on each side and one here to guard the horses, and the first man that comes out, you can all pull down on him . . . and, if he don't halt when I order, you can shoot. But if he gits inside that cabin, it'll be a long siege at best, because she's mighty nigh bulletproof."

They separated then, Grimes and Winchester going up one ridge, and Meshackatee and Hall up the other. As the sun began to shine on the bald slopes to the west, they settled down to watch the house. It had been built all too evidently for purposes of defense, although no loopholes appeared in the walls, but no windows appeared, either, and the door was of heavy oak slabs. The Texans were safe as long as they remained inside of it, and they seemed in no hurry to come out. A shrewd suspicion was beginning to form in Hall's mind that in some way their presence had been discovered, but they waited patiently until the sun was an hour high, and then a tall cowboy stumbled out. He was a typical Texan, all boots and high hat, and he headed for the woodpile without so much as a glance at the sinister hillsides above him.

"Put 'em up!" bellowed Meshackatee as the Texan reached for the axe, but instead the man started to run. He did not even look up, simply bolted for the doorway like a rabbit caught away from his hole. But the posse had been watching, and, as he started for the door, their rifles all spoke at once. The pile of chips at his feet seemed to leap into the air as the bullets struck all around him, but he escaped by some miracle and slammed the door behind him, at which Meshackatee ripped out a great oath.

"Come out of that cabin!" he roared from his hiding place, "come out, or we'll blow you to hell!"

But the men inside the cabin were punching loopholes through the chinks and Meshackatee opened fire. The work on the loopholes was given over precipitately, for the heavy bullets bored their way through the chinks, and, when a couple of explosive bullets almost blew down the door, the Texans were ready for a parley.

"Who air you fellers, anyway?" one shouted through the

doorway. "We're all right! We ain't done nothin'!"

"We're a posse of deputy sheriffs and you're wanted for horse stealing. Come out," thundered Meshackatee, "or we'll kill ye!"

"You'll kill us anyway!" answered the other of the men, and they went to work on their loopholes.

"I'll fix 'em," announced Meshackatee, and, slipping in another explosive bullet, he fired it through the hole in the door. There was a crash inside and a loud yell of protest, and then, very reluctantly, the shattered door was thrown open and the Texans stepped out with hands up.

"Come up here!" ordered Meshackatee over the top of a rock. "Is there anybody else in there?"

"Nope, the other boys are gone," answered one of the trembling prisoners. Both were both barely out of their teens, and Hall quickly searched them for concealed guns.

"All right," he said, "you can put down your hands. Come on, we'll go back to camp."

They returned to the horses, where Bill had a fire going and a pot of coffee on the coals, and Grimes and Winchester joined them.

"You sure ruined that cabin," observed Winchester to Meshackatee, but Grimes strode over to the prisoners.

"Oho," he said, "so you're the young bucks that have been raising all this deviltry. Well, we'll just make you an example for the rest of 'em to look at when they come over to steal our stock."

He made gruesome motions of tightening a loop about his neck and the Texans turned deathly pale.

"I thought you were deputies," said of one them at length, but no one responded directly. With two prisoners on their hands they would be handicapped at every turn, and the question before them was whether to let Grimes hang them or allow them to go scotfree.

"Well, what you got to say for yourselves?" asked Meshacka-tee at length, after they had eaten a scanty breakfast. "Where'd you git that band of horses you had yesterday?"

The younger of the boys was by now too scared to talk, but the older one spoke up boldly.

"We were coming in from Holbrook," he said, "and some men that we met said they'd give us ten dollars to drive these bronc's down into the basin."

"Come from Texas?" inquired Meshackatee. "Well, couldn't you see by them brands that half those horses was stolen? I know you could now, son, so don't make us hang you for a liar."

"You're a liar yourself!" flashed back the boy indignantly. "Didn't you claim you was a deputy sheriff!"

"Take the witness." Meshackatee shrugged, rolling his eyes at Winchester. "He's too danged smart for me."

"Lookee here, kid," began Winchester with a placating smile, "you'd better come through with the truth. Who're you working for . . . Isham Scarborough?"

"Don't know him," denied the boy. "We were jest rambling through the country when we met up with them fellers with the horses. Say, are you deputy sheriffs? Well then, you don't dare to hang me! Don't I git a trial, or nothing?"

"You're gitting a trial, right now," returned Winchester. "And if you git too gay, we'll jest take off these tin stars and show you whether or not we can hang you. You're a tough little devil, I can see that with one eye, but . . . oh, hell, let the little whelp go."

He laughed shortly and turned away, pretending to adjust his pistol, and Hall nodded at Meshackatee.

"We're not fighting boys," he said, but Grimes took the opposite view.

"Now, gentleman," he objected, rising up from where he sat,

"I think you're wrong, dead wrong. These boys may be young, but they knew what they were doing, and this stealing has got to stop, that's all. I'll jest take off this star, so they won't be no complications, and you can turn them over to me."

"No, don't you do it, mister!" cried the boy in a panic, running to cling to Meshackatee's knees. "I . . . I'll never steal another horse again. And this other boy, he's only a kid . . . we ran away from home together."

"Oh, I see," mumbled Meshackatee, and glanced questioningly at Grimes who stood with his lips grimly pursed.

"Well?" he demanded, but Meshackatee shook his head.

"Nope," he said, "they's too small, Mister Grimes. And I ran away from home myself."

"Then I resign," snarled Grimes, beginning to unpin his star, and Meshackatee held out his hand.

"Gimme the star, then," he replied, "you're too rough-shod for us. We didn't come out here to hang any kids. We came to git Isham Scarborough."

Grimes paused and rolled his evil eyes on the boys, then snapped his badge back in place.

"I'll stick," he said. "You're chicken-hearted, but I'll stick. But if these kids turn up later with a gang of their confederates, don't say I didn't warn ye!"

"Very well, Mister Grimes," returned Meshackatee politely, "and being as you're so *bravo*, we'll jest head back for the basin and put you up against some grown men."

CHAPTER TWENTY-ONE

If it was madness for Meshackatee and his posse of four to ride back into the stronghold of the Scarboroughs, there was a method in the madness. The Scarboroughs would be swarming like a nest of red ants on account of the killing of Red; they would be scouring the country and watching every trail, but, even so, a man must eat. Maverick Basin was the hold-out of a gang of men so desperate that they set all law at defiance, shooting down whoever opposed them, but it had a store, full of flour and bacon, and Meshackatee's packs were flat. First he had shared his food with Hall, and then with the Bassetts, and finally with Grimes and the boy horse thieves, and, when they turned back, there was nothing in the kaks but coffee and cartridges and tobacco.

They took to the high ground, led by Winchester Bassett who had ranged the whole country with his hounds, and at evening they emerged on a wooded hilltop and looked out at the basin with their glasses. The sun had hardly set when they rode out from cover and headed straight for the darkened store. The storekeeper was a careful, not to say a stingy, man, and he had his reasons also for preferring to sit in the dark, since bright windows have often drawn bullets. He was hiding when they rode up, but, finding his store surrounded, he lit up and opened the door.

"Oh, good evening." He cringed as Meshackatee loomed up before him. "Well, well, howdy do, Meshackatee."

"I want some grub," returned Meshackatee, "and I want it quick, without any high signs to the Scarboroughs. So jest git out your pencil and keep tally on what we take . . . you'll be paid by Tonto County."

"But the county is practically bankrupt," protested Johnson in an ague.

"So'm I," replied Meshackatee, "and I'm hungry to boot. So use your own judgment, Mister Johnson."

He stepped into the storeroom and began to hand out the sacks of flour, and after a glaring silence Mr. Johnson saw the point and began sullenly to check up the requisition. For a requisition it was, such as armies are wont to make, and deputy sheriffs in pursuit of criminals, and soon bacon and coffee and beans came out to fill the sacks that they slung on the saddles of their spare mounts.

"Now, what's the news, Mister Johnson?" spoke up Meshackatee abruptly. "Who's over at the Scarborough place now?"

"Why . . . *er* . . . Elmo," began the storekeeper, "and Miz Zoolah, of course."

"Where's Isham?" demanded Meshackatee, and the others stopped to listen, but Johnson only shook his head.

"He's gone," he said, and Meshackatee drew his big six-shooter and laid it down impressively in the lamplight.

"Gone where?" he asked, but not even the gun could make the frightened storekeeper tell.

"I don't know, boys, I swear it," he answered as they faced him, "but they say he's over in New Mexico. Been gone for a week, and now that Red is dead, young Elmo has taken things in charge."

"How many men has he got?" inquired Grimes, moving closer, and the storekeeper backed away instinctively.

"Oh, a great many!" he exclaimed. "Sometimes as much as forty. They're coming in all the time. This evening there were two all the way from Kentucky. . . ."

"What were their names?" broke in Hall, and the storekeeper winced.

"Why . . . er . . . Randolph," he said, "and, now that you speak of it, I believe they were inquiring for you."

"Very likely," replied Hall, and slipped quietly outside, where he could think what this meant to him. So Allifair's brothers had come! The feud of Tug Fork had been transplanted to Maverick Basin—the Randolphs had come to kill him. He stood in the shadows, looking out across the plain to where the lights of the Rock House still glowed. It was too late now; he had lost. Cal and Ewing were there, and, as soon as they learned the country, they would take up his trail like bloodhounds. They would follow him like a deer and like a deer he must flee, for Allifair loved her brothers. Bloody-handed as they were, and rough and brutal, she loved Cal and Ewing for what they might have been if the feud had not warped their whole lives. They were man-killers now, thin-lipped and cruel-eyed, and yet he dared not oppose them. Once more he must play the coward.

While the others lingered on, indulging in a few drinks and cross-questioning the reluctant Mr. Johnson, he sorted out a pack load of the most substantial food and lashed it on his spare horse. He was mounting to go when Winchester Bassett stepped out, followed by Bill, carrying a big sack of food.

"Why, hello," exclaimed Winchester, "are you going to leave us? We're going up north and lay for Isham."

"Yes, I've got to go," said Hall, "but don't tell the storekeeper. The Randolphs have come out here to kill me."

"I had an idee they had," admitted Winchester. "Well, sorry to see you go. But say, wait a minute and you can start off with me and Bill . . . that storekeeper is a Scarborough spy."

Hall waited, still in the shadows, for the light from the store door might reveal his presence to his enemies, and, as he watched the Rock House, he saw a lantern leave the house and go bobbing out to the barn. There was a hair-trigger atmosphere about the whole raid that set his jangled nerves on edge, for he knew that the Scarboroughs kept close watch over the store, even dictating who should come there for supplies. They would be riding over soon to see who had been there, if they were not already skulking nearby, and the news of his presence would be the signal for the Randolphs to take up the trail again. For years, back in Kentucky, they had dogged his tracks, trying to catch him for a moment off his guard, and he, throwing great circles, had often swung in behind them, so that they in turn were pursued. More than once he had ambushed them, and once he had shot Cal, but they had always crept away leaving the battle undecided, for the feud had taught the value of stealth. The men who fought in the open had long before been killed—it was Indian warfare now.

Bill and Winchester came out, after taking a last drink, and rode off in silence down the road. The night was still, so that the sounds traveled far, and the circumstances of their homecoming were depressing. Except for a few times when, at the risk of their lives, they had crept in to leave their mother some fresh beef, they had never been near the house since that fatal day when Sharps and old Henry had been killed. Old Susie had detected movements on the top of the hill where the Scarboroughs had once laid in wait, and Winchester and Bill had evidence of their own to show that the house was watched. It was the old system of the Scarboroughs, always to lie in wait and shoot down their enemies from the brush.

The hounds came rushing out at them, changing their baying to joyous yelps as they recognized their long-lost masters, and old Susie, for once, forgot her Indian stoicism and wept as she clung to Bill. He was her favorite boy, the baby she had carried when she had traveled overland in search of her husband, and, when they had put down her supplies and were preparing to go, she still clung desperately to Bill.

"You go on," he said to Winchester, "I'll stay with Maw a while. But I'll ketch you . . . get the boys and start ahead."

"Well, all right," grumbled Winchester, "but you be careful, kid, them Scarboroughs are on the prod."

They parted company at the gate, Winchester riding for the store and Hall turning off to the east, but, as he rode through the darkness, Hall halted on the trail, and at last he wheeled and turned back. The vague uneasiness that had held him all evening suddenly took form and clutched at his heart. What if the Randolphs had come, not to run him down and kill him, but to carry their sister away? He circled the basin and finally headed south, cutting across the open plain and taking shelter in the wooded hills beyond.

When the new day dawned, he crept out on a point where he could look down and see her from afar. She must know he was near, for the storekeeper had told him that he was believed to be the slayer of Red, and, if that was the case, how anxiously she must be waiting for the time when he would appear on the mound. How many times already she must have glanced out through the loophole, hoping to see his waiting form beneath the tree, and now he was slinking away, without even looking to the Providence he claimed as his guide. He focused his glasses and gazed down at the Rock House, and at daylight Allifair appeared.

She stepped to the doorway, dressed in white like a bride, although she was only a kitchen drudge, and her eyes seemed to be turned to the hills. Almost she seemed to see him, or to sense his distant presence, for she raised her hand in a sign, and then she waved him away, just as plainly as if she spoke to him, and turned sorrowfully back into the house. Soon the smoke from the huge chimney told the story of her industry—she was cooking while the rest of them slept. Hall watched them as they came out, Miz Zoolah and Elmo, and at last the men whom he never had feared—Cal Randolph and the tall, lanky Ewing. They were typical mountaineers in their high boots and slouched hats, and yet after all not so different from the Texans who came striding across from the bunkhouse. But he feared them now, for they had come to take his life and his hands were tied by love. They were the brothers of Allifair and she had beckoned him away, yet he lingered, waiting to see their next move.

A dozen rash plans leaped up in his brain—to steal her and bear her away, to hide her from their fury and then return to Tug Fork, to put an end to the feud. But each time the vision of Cal and Ewing Randolph rose up to brand them as worse than dreams; the fate that had pursued him was still on his trail; nothing could be done while her brothers were there. He put down his glasses and gazed out across the basin, seeking some end to the *fantasma* of his life. Even here, as in Kentucky, it had been a nightmare of death and violence, while his heart was sick for peace. All he wanted was peace, the same surcease we give the dead—a forgetting, oblivion, a new life. Yet even after one death his incognito had been discovered and the chase was on again. Nothing would stay the dark passions of the men he had warred against; they were ruthless as death itself.

He closed his eyes wearily to shut out the sight of this valley that had once seemed so fair, and sleep swooped to seize him in an instant. But while his senses swooned, something came to his ears that roused him as nothing else could—a rifle shot, far away. He listened, half convinced, and a volley ripped the air like the tearing of a strip of rough cloth. It came from the hill, where the Scarboroughs had hidden before, the hill that looked down on the Bassetts'. But why did they shoot when Sharps and Henry were both dead, and Winchester and Bill . . . ? His

147

heart stopped and leaped again, and he knew the answer. Bill Bassett had stayed too long.

CHAPTER TWENTY-TWO

There never was a feud, nor yet a war, that did not revert to barbarism, for reprisal invites reprisal, and hot blood breeds new excesses until it ends in a mad swirl of killing. Always the human reason, ever the servant to our passions, finds a way to justify the slaughter. For the object of warfare, of course, is to kill, and why stop short of the absolute? Why leave boys to grow to manhood, or women to breed more boys, or old men to nurse the spark of future wars: why not kill them all, as speedily as possible, and with the least possible danger to ourselves? There we have the justification not only of war, but of feuds and murder from ambush, but the murders come first and reason follows tardily to lull the protests of conscience.

Hall McIvor had killed from ambush, and had been shot down in turn, but the thought of Bill's death, conjured up by the rifle shots, left him sick at the savagery of it all. By a process of reasoning he had brought himself to join this war, in order to end yet another war, but until the last Scarborough, or the last Bassett, was dead, he knew there would be no end. And was it far-fetched to kill off the Scarboroughs in order to save the McIvors and Randolphs? He lay hidden on his high point like a lion that hears the dogs, undecided whether to stand fast or flee. If he fled, they would pursue him—but did he not have a covert? And if he stayed, they would send him after Bill. It was a fight to the finish, and yet no fight of his, if only he could take Allifair and escape.

But this was not the time to put their fortunes to the test; he must wait till her brothers were gone. The war was on in Kentucky and they could not be spared long—but when they went, they would take Allifair with them! Back to the battle-ground along the Big Sandy, ten times as blood-soaked as here, and there they would guard her like a criminal. For that was the worst crime they knew, to wish to marry a McIvor. No, the time to rescue Allifair was now. But first he must return to his castle in the cliff and prepare it for her coming.

He rode cautiously for two nights, hiding on flat mountain-tops by day, and found a way at last up the chasm, which was roaring now with water. The summer rains had come, turning the ravines into torrents and Turkey Creek into a river, and whatever tracks he made were soon washed away, leaving him lost to all the world. He hobbled his horses on the flat below him, where he could guard them from his cave above, and, working feverishly, he bore his provisions up the trail and made camp that night by his castle. The court was broad enough, and the smoke from his fire sucked back through the high, gloomy passageway; he made a couch of his lion-skin, flung down in the open, leaving the mud-sealed door unbroken.

Perhaps the imprint in the mud of a hand like a woman's held him back from violating the sanctuary, but in the morning he breached the door, for he, too, had a woman and the dead must give way to the living. The mate of his mountain lion was still prowling about, and must Allifair lack shelter and retreat from wild animals in order that the dead should sleep undis-turbed? He smashed his way in ruthlessly and entered the burial chamber, which was low and dark as a tomb. It had been a dwelling once—there was soot on the rafters and a fireplace over in the corner—but now it was smothered beneath the dust of countless centuries, as fine and impalpable as flour. It rose up at every step, almost choking him with its saltiness and its odor of things long dead, and the sarcophagus against the wall was blanketed over as if with a fall of snow.

At one end of the burial mound he found an *olla* full of corn left to nourish the departing spirit on its journey, and at the other a second *olla* with only a watermark to show where the spirits had drunk, but the thing that impressed him most was a huge bulk against the cliff, an *olla* nearly as high as a man. It, too, was blanketed in dust and its broad top was sealed, as if to protect some great treasure, but the treasures of the cliff-dwellers could wait. What he wanted was their room, to shelter his lady from the mountain lions. He tied together a bundle of switches and began to sweep out the dust, dashing out from time to time to get air, and, as he was brushing down the walls, he discovered a blackened hole in the corner above the fire. This, too, was sealed with mud, but when he punched it clear, the clouds of stinging dust went swirling up and out, leaving the chamber of the cliff-dwellers clear.

So it had been long centuries before, when these dead had still lived and cooked their corn on the flat stones below, for the draft through the low doorway sucked up past the fireplace and went out at the smoke vent above. Hall set to work again, clearing away the mound with its crumbling skeleton, its prayer sticks and arrows and clubs, but when he came to the great *olla*, he found it sunk into the floor and as immovable as the cliff itself. He tried to pierce the seal, but it was another *olla*, set down over the greater one below, and finally, seizing a club, he smashed in the top, only to start back at the sound of a splash. So this was the treasure the cliff-dwellers had concealed, and yet what treasure was greater? He leaned over the broad rim and tasted the water doubtfully—it was sweet as if it flowed from a spring! But certainly, if it had been stored for centuries and centuries, it would be flat and tainted by the pottery. He splashed it over the rim, wetting down the parched dirt floor, but the water in the basin did not lower. It was a spring walled up and cupped in the *ollas,* a dimpling fount for Allifair.

Hall wet down the floor and swept it out again, letting it air until the room was sweet and clean, and then in mad haste he set to work to bring in wood and make a bed of dry grass. He stored his provisions against the wall, and threw down the lion skin by the fire, and, closing the doorway, ran down to catch his horses, for the time for action had come. Here was their dwelling place at last, all set and waiting, lacking only the smile of Allifair to give it the glow of home. As he spurred back over the trail, dragging the led horse behind him, he envisioned her sitting by the fireplace. Although the night was dark and the trails sluiced out by rain, when the day dawned, he was hidden in the hills where he could look down and watch for Allifair.

She appeared with the dawn, still clad in white, and stood poised against the blackness of the doorway, but this time she did not wave, just stood gazing at the hills until abruptly she turned and went in. Hall was hidden in a thicket of bristling manzanita on the brow of a pine-clad ridge, and his horses, staked and hobbled, were concealed in a hollow where he could keep them under his eye. He slept, for no man could creep up to his hiding place without snapping a thousand rough twigs, and, when he awoke, it was raining again and the thunder was rolling along the hills. Taking shelter beneath a tree, he threw his slicker over his shoulders and watched the swift rush of the clouds, the lightning that flashed and stabbed, making the earth tremble at its shock, until at last the great pageant rolled past. The sun came out warm, gleaming like silver from the thunderheads, and down at the Rock House men mounted dancing ponies and went scampering away up the trail.

Hall counted them as they went, eleven cowboys in all, and, as he spied a great horse herd trotting in from the north, he guessed the cause of their haste. This was another of those bands of Mormon horses, taken by force from the ranchers above the Mogollon Rim, and, unless he was mistaken, the Avenging Angels from Mountain Meadow would not be far behind. They would come riding as before, disguised as raiding Apaches with horse tails and handkerchiefs on their heads, and every man at the Rock House would be needed that night to hold the herd against them. There might even be a fight, for the Mormons were determined—and while they were drawn away, he could ride to the Rock House and steal Allifair in spite of them.

The sun went down behind a bank of angry clouds, every streamed in the basin was awash, and the rumble of the distant waters told of greater floods to be crossed if they endeavored to escape across Turkey Creek. But no sooner was it night than he rode boldly down the ridge, leaving his horses just behind the Indian mound. Men were dashing to and fro, but something bade him be venturesome, and he stood out boldly against the sky, then he crouched back and waited, for the dogs had begun to bark, and at last she came running up the path. They did not stop, even for a lover's kiss, but hurried away down the hill, and hardly had they left the Rock House behind them than they heard the hue and cry. It started at the house with a succession of six pistol shots and Hall swung from the trail to let the chase go by, for he heard them coming after them.

They had started down the main trail to Jump-Off Point, but now he turned east and circled back to the north, with Allifair close behind him. She, too, had brought a slicker to protect her from the rain, and beneath her man's hat she looked no different from the cowboys who were scouring the trails in search of them. They rode at a trot as if going to the horse herd and a galloping Texan, riding back to the house, held up his hand as he went splashing by. But that way was too dangerous and Hall turned to the east, taking the trail that led to the Bassetts'.

A black cloud that blotted the east twinkled with flares of heat lightning, the stars seemed to swim through a mist, and, as the Bassett dogs rushed out, they veered sharply away, taking the trail that led down to Turkey Creek. But there they stopped short for the water, in the pale starlight, seemed to be rushing with resistless force. It rose up in huge waves, smooth and slick as a ground swell but with logs and writhing branches in its grip, and, where it crossed the riffles, it roared with shuddering thunder and threw up a white comb of foam.

"Can we cross it?" she asked at last, and he shrugged his shoulders.

"Do you dare to try?" he countered.

"I'll follow you anywhere!" she answered, and took off her slicker, but he sat on his horse, irresolute.

The very rocks at the bottom of the stream seemed to be grinding and rumbling beneath the flood, and yet in his time he had crossed worse torrents than this, although once he had nearly been drowned.

"Can you swim?" he asked, and, when she shook her head, he turned and looked back across the plain. With the creek roaring in front of them not a hoof beat could be heard, but he pictured it swarming with horsemen. They would be spurring to the south, knowing that was where they would flee, but others would be coming to the east, and sooner or later he would have to make a fight, for Miz Zoolah would never give up. She would send out every man, if they had to abandon the horse herd, to scour the country for Allifair, and, compared to what would follow, if he had to give them battle, the creek did not seem so terrible. Its roar was no more than the rush of water past rough snags, the passing of sand waves through the crests, and, if worst came to worst, he might reach her and save her if their horses went down among the rocks.

"Keep your horse's head upstream," he said at last, "and rein him in if he falls, but if he goes down in spite of you, try to catch him by the tail, and in that way he may drag you ashore."

He leaned over and kissed her. Then, with a last touch of the hand, he edged his horse into the stream. The water was deep, for it was just above a riffle where the flood went pouring over a bar, and, as his horse stepped into a hole, it plunged and half fell, then rose up and tried to turn back. But Hall only reined him lower, just above the roaring thunder and the splash and spume of the bar, and close behind Allifair's mount followed after him, feeling its way along the treacherous bottom. Hall's horse went down again and came up swimming, only to find himself across the main channel, and, seeing Hall land on the other side, Allifair plunged in after him, coming out in a shower of flying mud. A huge, branching tree bobbed solemnly down the current, swinging about as if to brush them from their foothold, but now the horses were struggling, as eager to get across as before they had been loath to go in. They progressed in great leaps, in swift scramblings and terrifying lunges, and finally, all atremble, they waded out through the shallows and stood limply on the opposite side. The tree swept on past, logs and driftwood bobbed and curtsied, the sand waves roared terribly through the crests, but now it all seemed good for it raised a barrier behind them that the hardiest would hesitate to cross. Hall reined his horse into the washed-out, rocky trail, and they began the long ride to Cold Spring.

CHAPTER TWENTY-THREE

In ancient days, before taking any action, men stopped to consult an oracle or looked for omens in the flight of birds, but now, with equal results, we make our own auguries and follow what we call a psychic hunch. If we feel lucky, we play, and, if we feel unlucky, we quit, and no system has been devised that will bring better results, for all that the fortune-tellers say. Hall had felt a strong hunch the moment he smashed in the sealed *olla* and found it a fountain of water; it had seemed an intervention, an interposition of that Providence that he believed had raised him from the dead. The hand that he could not see seemed to be leading him again, where before all had been darkness and doubt, to be smoothing out his way and solving the difficulties that before had seemed insuperable. And if it could give him water and a shelter for his beloved, then surely it could guide his footsteps and so order his goings and comings that he would succeed at last in his quest.

All that night as he rode on, with Allifair close behind, he was conscious of a hand that led him on, and at daylight, when he rode down to the crossing at Cold Spring, he did not hesitate to plunge into the flood. Their horses were weak and the creek was still high, but they fought their way through anyhow and led their mounts up the chasm without a slip or a fall. It was a miracle of good luck, and, as they took shelter in the cave, the rain clouds lowered as if to cover them. The lightning began to play a weird devil's dance along the summit of the eastern ridge, the thunder smote their crags and called for rain, and, as they stood in the court of their castle in the air, they saw their pursuers ride into the cañon below.

They were weary and bedraggled but still leaning beside their saddle horns to trace the line of horse tracks through the mud, a band of four horsemen, shrouded to the chin in sluicing slickers but following grimly on their trail. Who they were they could not tell in the blinding rain, but, as they gazed over their rampart, they saw one essay the crossing and go down as if he had stepped into a well. The others shook out their ropes and rode to his rescue, dragging horse and man to the shore, and then in disgust they rode up to the low cliff-dwellings and took shelter from the fury of the storm. Hall glanced down at Allifair who stood clutching his hand, and they turned back and entered their new home.

She had held out bravely but now she sank down, bereft of the last of her strength, and, after he had made a fire, Hall spread her bed beside it, for she was drenched and chilled to the bone. He boiled coffee over the fireplace and held a cupful to her lips, and, after she had drunk, she opened her eyes and lay gazing at the strange, tomb-like dwelling. No light came in except through the low doorway, the fire cast strange shadows among the rafters, and yet somehow she felt a sweet contentment steal over her as she watched her lover by the fire. He was there, he would provide for her, and no one would ever find them—they were hidden away like twin eagles.

She fell into a deep sleep, and, when she awoke, he was standing above her, smiling. Food was simmering on the fire, but there was rain on his hat and he had brought in the breath of outdoors.

"They are looking for us," he said, and smiled again. "But they'll never find us here."

"No, not here," she answered, and sat up quickly for he had

laid a young turkey by the fire.

"Oh, did you shoot it?" she cried, and he stooped down and kissed her, then lifted her quickly to her feet.

"No, sweetheart." He laughed. "I didn't dare to shoot, but I drove it into my trap. And while you were asleep, I took our horses up the chasm and hid them in a little lost valley. Now all we have to do is to keep out of sight and let the chase go by."

He drew her closer to him, and she leaned against his breast, smiling softly as he told her of his love, and then they sat down to their first meal together while the storm swept by outside. Nothing mattered to them now; they were sheltered and warmed and fed, and their dream had at last come true. Far into the night, although sleep made them nod, they sat up and talked of the past. Hall spoke of the time when he had seen her first, when he had crept to the Randolphs' very door, and how she had saved him from Ewing and Cal when a word would have meant his death. And from there they drifted on through the maze of their wanderings, since she, like a culprit, had been sent to Arizona and he had followed on her trail. It was a tale of true love, in which neither had ever wavered, until now in the chamber of some ancient cliff-dweller they sat nodding by their fire.

They slept then at last, and in the morning the bright sunshine shot a shaft of golden light through the door. All the great world without was awake and on the move, but Nature had demanded its toll—and, when Hall roused up, their broad cave was in the shadow and the sun had passed over the crags. He stepped softly to the rampart and looked down into the cañon, where the creek was still roaring in flood, and up and down its course, for he could view it for miles, he saw trailers, out cutting for sign. There was a fire in the fireplace when he came back from his watch, but, after they had eaten, he covered it with ashes lest the odor of the smoke betray them. They settled down in the broad court, watching their pursuers from the protecting darkness and talking tranquilly as the search went on, and, when evening came on, they leaned over the low wall and gazed down at the camp by Cold Spring.

More men had come in, until now there were ten of them, and the flame of their campfire illuminated the windows of the lower cliff-dwellings until they glowed like the portholes of a fort. Even their voices could be heard above the rush of the flood, which had subsided to a tumbling stream. But seeing their pursuers below only added to their contentment and they found time to look up at the stars. It was a soft and balmy night and no lions were abroad to waken the echoes with their yells; all their world seemed at peace, and yet now there fell a silence in which each followed out his own thoughts. The past was not enough, nor yet the tranquil present, but each must quest on into the future.

"When these men have all gone," spoke up Allifair at last, "and my brothers have given up the search, shall we . . . I mean . . . well, what do you plan to do then?"

"What is there to do," answered Hall, "except to work out our destiny? But how we can be married is more than I know. Are you brave enough to stay here alone?"

"Alone," she repeated with a catch in her voice, and then she reached for his hand. "No, Hall," she said, "we are too happy, you must not leave me. But I am brave enough to go with you . . . anywhere."

"Ours is always the hardest way," he said. "Have you thought what is going to become of us? Every day that I stay here, I shall eat up by so much the food that should be kept to feed you, and, when that is gone, can you live on turkeys and acorns, as I was compelled to do for days?"

"I can do what you can do," she answered resolutely. "But why do you have to go? Why can't we stay here together until the search for us is over . . . ?"

"Because," he broke in gently, "we are living in the world, and you know what people will say."

"Yes, I know." She sighed. "But why can't we be married? Why can't we ride into Tonto as soon as they leave and be married and start back home?"

"Because the trails will be watched, and your brothers will kill me if they ever find us together."

"Not if we're married!" she protested, but he took her in his arms and his silence questioned even that.

"They are hard men," he said, "and they came out here to kill me . . . but behind it all is your aunt. She told you in my presence that she would rather shoot you down than see you married to a McIvor, and I believe, Allifair, she would do it. But here you will be safe, and, when I have finished with Isham. . . ."

"Oh, Hall," she reproached, "can't you learn to forgive? Does all that I have suffered count for nothing? I read killing in your eyes, that day that Sharps was shot . . . but I'll never forgive you if you do. You are determined to kill Isham, I know by your silence, but think what it means to me. He is my uncle after all, because he married Aunt Zoolah, and the McIvors have killed enough of my kin. But it isn't that alone. I want you to stop killing, and the only time to stop is now."

"God knows . . . ," began Hall, and then he paused and sighed. "I am weary of this killing," he said. "God only knows how sick of it I am, but a man must keep his self-respect. I would give my right hand if the circumstances could be different, but it's either him or me. I can forgive him for myself, but for what he has done to others . . . well, we won't talk about it any more, dear."

"Yes we will," she answered back, "because I won't marry a murderer . . . and that's what you are at heart. Not that I blame you for it, Hall, for I know how you were brought up. All I ask is that now you should stop. Is that too much to ask?"

"No, not too much at all," he replied at length, "provided your uncle will stop. I fled like a coward when I heard your brothers had come, because I would rather be killed than kill them, but I ask you, is it right that I should promise to spare Isham when he is hunting me everywhere like an animal? Who is paying those men who are camped down below us? I tell you they have chased me far enough."

His voice was tense with passion and he drew his hand away, but she reached out and caught it back.

"Hall, dear," she pleaded, "don't you know what I mean? I'm afraid that Isham will kill you."

He laughed softly as she kissed him and crept back into his arms, where she shuddered and laid her head on his breast.

"No," he said, "he will never kill me. I've got too much to live for now."

CHAPTER TWENTY-FOUR

The chase, which had been flung far, swung back toward Dead-man Cañon, where the trail of the fugitives had disappeared, and with the others came the Randolphs and Isham Scarborough, riding up the creek from Tonto. Apache trailers came drifting in, drawn like vultures by the crowd, and soon, under their guidance, the search party crossed the creek and came out on the bench below the castle. Hall and Allifair could hear their shouts as they found the marks of his first turkey trap in the underbrush above the little spring, and then the chase led on to the cliff-dwellings below them, where Hall had made camp the first time. But the signs were all old and they came back to the spring, where they could look up and see the lost castle. Every word that they said could be heard now perfectly and Allifair trembled as she listened.

"Well, the house is there, ain't it?" argued Isham, trying to bully the Apache trailers. "How'd they git up to it? Well, *busca* the trail!"

"No! No tlail!" responded the Apaches, and that was the last heard of them, for the cowboys had taken sides on the matter. Some swore that the trail came down from the top, and that they could see a kind of bear track down the cleft, and the others were just as positive that it had ascended the cliff but had been lost by a cave-in of the rock.

"No! No tlail!" repeated the Apaches when the uproar had subsided, and Isham Scarborough came back at them angrily.

"You're scairt, you black rascals!" he shouted. "Hey, Charley . . . you take me up that mountain? Well, there, now, you see? These danged Injuns are buffaloed. They're afraid Old Man Baker will kill 'em!"

"No! No 'flaid!" grunted the Indians, but they would not go up the chasm, for no Apache ever set foot on Baker Mountain.

"Hey, I'll tell you!" hollered Isham, his voice rising above the Babel like the roar of a mountain bull. "I'll tell you where they've gone! Up Devil's Chasm and plumb over the summit. They couldn't get nowhere else! Didn't we trail 'em to the crick, and ain't we rode clean to Tonto, cutting circles to pick up their tracks? Well, they crossed then, I'm telling ye, even if you fellers couldn't, and by this time they're clean to Geronimo!"

"Well, let's go to Geronimo, then," spoke up Cal Randolph's even voice, "what's the use of trying to climb this mountain?"

"They may be hid up there!" cried Isham. "But cripes, boys, we know one thing. They never went down that crick. And if they didn't go there, where else could they go except . . . ?"

He paused as a voice began shouting his name, and Hall peeped over the rampart. A man had ridden down to their camp across the creek and was waving his hat and hallooing.

"What d'ye want?" demanded Isham, walking to the edge of the bench and looking across at the runner. "What's the matter with you, anyhow?"

"Your wife says to come home!" shouted the messenger. "They's been a big raid. All your horses are run off! And three of the boys was found hung!"

"Hung!" echoed Isham, and every man in the party jumped up and ran to the rim.

"What's that?" they clamored, and Hall and Allifair rose up to catch the startling news.

"Why, they was night riders," explained the runner. "They

wore masks and dressed like Injuns! Yes, come in at night and caught three boys standing guard! We found them hung to a tree! And they run off all your horses!"

"Hell's fire!" exclaimed Isham, and stood staring across the cañon while his men gathered together in groups.

"That was that sheepman, Grimes," whispered Hall to Allifair. "He's organized all those Mormons above the Mogollon Rim."

"Oh, will he come down here?" asked Allifair aghast. "Because Ewing and Cal. . . ."

"Maybe they'll leave now," suggested Hall, and they listened again, for Isham was beginning to shout.

"Which way'd they go?" he inquired, and, when the man answered north, he burst into a fit of cursing. "It's them dadburned Mormon ranchers!" he exclaimed, and started back for his horse. "Well, let's go, boys," he said, when they had gathered by the spring, "we can tend to McIvor afterward. But if anyone wants to stay here, I'll give one thousand dollars to the man that brings me his hair. He's the dirty, dog-goned rascal that stirred up all this ruckus, but I can't stop to monkey with him now. Come on, Cal, ain't you coming with me?"

"No," answered Cal's voice and then, after a silence, "we didn't come out here to help you steal horses."

"Oh, you didn't, eh?" railed Isham, his voice tense with excitement. "Well, since when have you got to be so good? Jest the minute they's any trouble. . . ."

"We come out here to get our sister," broke in Ewing's high voice. "And we're going to hunt till we find her."

"Well, hunt and be damned to ye!" burst out Isham in a fury, and went spurring off down the trail. His cowboys followed after him, talking low among themselves, and Hall and Allifair crouched down and listened.

"Well?" spoke up the voice they recognized as Cal's, but Ewing did not reply. "Let's ask these Indians," went on Cal, "maybe they know of some trail. Hey," he called, "come over here!"

"What you want?" demanded an Indian in arrogant tones, and Cal asked about the trail up the chasm. "No good!" replied the Apache. "Go hup steep! Go hup mo', mo' steep! Bimby too steep, fall down. Me no likum. Go home."

"Where you think this man go?" spoke up Ewing. "You find him, we give you two hundred dollars."

There was a guttural conversation in Apache then, and Allifair began to cry softly, but Hall was listening over the wall. If the Apaches took up his trail, they would undoubtedly find his horses and his turkey traps and saddles, too. They might even find the entrance to their cave, with results he did not care to contemplate, for he could not kill the Randolphs and they were sworn to kill him—but fate turned the shaft away. The Indians were afraid of Old Man Baker and his mountain and they revised their opinions to suit.

"Go hon . . . down wate'," answered the spokesman at last. "Fall in, maybeso both dlown. How much you give . . . findum body?"

"Nothing!" burst out Cal. "Go on away, you dirty devil. By God, Ewing, I believe he's right."

"Well, I told ye!" accused Ewing, his voice high and complaining. "I told you we hadn't ought to come! But you had to have your way, and now who's going to face Dad . . . ?"

"*Aw,* hush up!" returned Cal impatiently.

"You give coffee?" asked the Indian with painful distinctness, and Cal flew into a fury.

"No, damn ye!" he cursed. "Git away, before I kill ye. Come on, Ewing, let's quit and go home."

There was a silence then, broken by sonorous Apache as the Indians talked on gravely among themselves, and finally, across the creek, Hall saw the Texans riding north and the Randolphs heading for Tonto. Then he stooped and gathered up Allifair, who had given herself over to weeping, and carried her into the house.

"I can't help it," she sobbed. "They're all so rough and brutal, and they curse and . . . oh, I just hate them! And to think of Cal and Ewing offering two hundred dollars. . . ."

"And they'd have found us, too." Hall nodded as he put her down onto the ground. "But God looks after His own. I believe He is saving us, to work His will elsewhere. I'll never doubt it again. When I came here to look for you, I was sure of my mission. I knew He was leading me to you, and I knew that somehow we should manage to escape, and be united, and unite our own people. But afterward, when I was hiding like a rabbit among the rocks and the Scarboroughs were prospering so wonderfully, well, I couldn't believe it, it didn't seem possible, it hardly seems possible now. But hatred raises up hatred until it destroys itself, and now this sheepman, Grimes, whose herders they killed, has descended like a destroying angel upon them. It will all work out now, and when I come back. . . ."

"Are you going?" she asked suddenly, standing bolt upright. "Oh, Hall, I want you . . . here with me. I'll live on acorns. I'll do anything. Won't you stay?"

"I'll be back soon," he said, and turned away.

Chapter Twenty-Five

There was a day of anxious waiting when they sat and watched the trails, and then, in the twilight, Hall led Allifair up the chasm and showed her how to bait and set his traps. He helped her gather acorns, carried in a last load of wood, and, late in the evening, they parted. She was brave again now, although she still hoped he would relent, but the traditions of a lifetime were behind his resolve and he left her without a tremor. Even his last kiss seemed cold, as if his mind had leaped ahead and was held by the grim task before him, and his voice, when he spoke, had the sternness of an ascetic who has banished all weakness from his life.

"I must go," he said, "and fight this out with Isham, and they will hunt me through the hills like a wild animal. And your part is to stay here, like a wild animal, too, hidden away where no one can find you. But this is our last trial, and, when I come back, I hope it will be with honor."

He left her then suddenly, before she could answer, and glided away into the darkness, and Allifair clutched the pistol, which he had given her for her safety, and returned to the eagles' nest alone. She was like an eagle now that has lost its chosen mate, and its power to fly as well, and, if he did not come back, she would be more than lost, for the world would be empty without him. Yet what he said was true—it was her part to wait. The rest was in the hands of God.

As for Hall, he rode forth cautiously, scouting around above the basin, until at last he was able to see that the Scarboroughs had taken cover—they were shut up within the Rock House. Around the bunkhouse and corrals the Texas gunmen swarmed like flies, but they did not ride abroad, not even to the store— except when someone had called. Then they rode over in threes and fours, probably to get the latest news as it was retailed by the inquisitive storekeeper. After waiting for two days, Hall rode off and on the fourth day he sighted Meshackatee, riding south at the head of a posse. But this was no posse of three or four fugitives, scouting anxiously through the hills; it numbered ten fighting men, and they rode down by the main trail from the north. Winchester Bassett was still with him and Grimes, the sheepman; the others were strangers to Hall.

"Hello!" hailed Meshackatee when Hall showed himself above them. "Come down and tell us what you know."

They halted on the trail, and, after Hall had shaken hands, Meshackatee drew him aside.

"Where you been?" he said. "Still gunning for Isham? Well, we've got him holed up like a fox. Grimes came down here last week with a bunch of Latter-Day Saints, and we busted him, by grab, over night. Or at least, Grimes did. I wasn't in on the deal . . . not officially. It was a dirty job, anyway . . . they hung that little kid that we caught up Horse-Thief Cañon. No, not the one that cried . . . that nervy little devil that stood up and told us where to go to. He was too damned nervy, that's the trouble."

"And are you going back?" demanded Hall, "to repeat the performance? Because if you are. . . ."

"Oh, no, no," protested Meshackatee, "that was too durned raw for me. And besides, I'm an officer of the law. This is a regularly appointed posse of deputy sheriffs, and we're going to serve a warrant on Isham."

"You'll never do it," declared Hall. "I've been watching him for two days and he never goes away from the Rock House. And he's got twenty-two men, not counting himself and Elmo. That bunch could stand off an army."

"Yes, they could," admitted Meshackatee, "they's no use denying it. But Grimes and his men are so crazy to git at him that Winchester and me have given up. They're going to storm that house, if it's the last act of their lives . . . unless we can tole Isham out. Say, there's an idee," he said, stopping to scratch his bearded chin. "I'll tell you how I believe we can work it. We can let you go in first, and, unless I'm greatly mistaken, he'll take after you like a bat out of hell."

"No he won't," returned Hall. "I know him too well. And besides, I've got a plan of my own. I don't want him to know I'm alive."

"No, but listen," insisted Meshackatee, "what do you care what he knows, as long as we git 'im between the eyes? We'll lay the ambush first and you lead him into it . . . we don't care, we'll take on the whole bunch of 'em!"

"Well," began Hall, and Meshackatee grabbed him by the shoulder.

"That's the talk," he said. "Come on."

"No, I don't agree to that," answered Hall, shaking him off. "But I tell you what I might do."

"Well, go ahead!" cried Meshackatee, dragging him back to the posse. "Hey, boys, here's a man we can rely on. Go ahead, Hall, and tell us your scheme."

"I've noticed," explained Hall as the posse gathered about him, "that all the Scarborough men keep close to the house. They're afraid to go out into the hills. But every time some neutral rides up to the store, they go over there, sooner or later, to get the news. Now, if you gentleman will conceal yourselves inside the foundation of that burned house. . . ."

"Hooray!" cheered Meshackatee, giving him a slap on the

Dane Coolidge

back. "I told you he'd think up some scheme. And in the morning you can show up in the open."

"I'll do more than that," answered Hall. "I'll ride in from the south . . . alone. They'd be sure to scent a trap if they saw me there already, but if I came in just at dawn, and rode away with some provisions, I feel sure that some of them would follow. There's a thousand dollars reward on my head."

"Aha!" cackled Grimes, who had been wagging his head in approval, "so that's how bad they want ye!"

"Yes," admitted Hall, "but that's the very reason why we'll never lure Isham himself. He'll hold back and let his gunmen do the riding."

"Well, we'll see," asserted Grimes, "and, if Isham don't come out, we'll damned sure go in there and git him. D'ye remember what I told you when he killed my boss herder? Well, I've got three of his cowboys already. And I ain't started, man, don't you never forgit that, nor these fellers here ain't started. Them Texans of his rode up to their ranches and took the work horses off of their plows. D'ye think they'll stand for that? Not while there's a man above the rim that can shoot."

"Well, come on," broke in Meshackatee, "we'd better git out of here before some neutral comes by and tips our hand. And to make it look convincing, in case anyone is watching, we'll turn around and ride back north."

He led the way up the cañon, and they camped in a pocket where they could waylay every man that passed by, but the times were troublous and not a soul came or went, to add to the Mormons' grim toll. They were frankly out for blood and Hall made no protest, even when Grimes taunted him about the boy they had hung. He was a boy, that was true, but he had not heeded their warning, and they had caught him red-handed again. Hall kept away from the posse, talking gravely with Winchester who was now the last of the Bassetts, and that

170

evening after dark they took the trail to Maverick Basin, surrounding the store an hour past midnight.

They found Johnson hiding in bed, trembling and begging for mercy, for he remembered the fate of three night-herding cowboys, and long before dawn they had schooled him in the part that he must act in the grim play to come. When Hall rode up, Johnson was to step out and meet him and stand talking so the Scarboroughs could see them, and then he was to retreat and come out with provisions, which were to be tied on the back of Hall's saddle. That was all, except at the end Johnson was to give the watching Scarboroughs a signal—and if the signal did not work, if the Scarboroughs refrained from coming, then the storekeeper was to be hung as a traitor. And the posse meant it, too, as Johnson soon divined, and, besides, he had seen the three cowboys that had been hanged.

Hall rode away north with the men who were to guard the horses, and, as the false dawn appeared, he took to the brush, coming out past the Bassett place at daylight. The hounds, as he had expected, suddenly rushed out at him baying, and, as he spurred rapidly away, they set up such a barking that the Scarborough dogs took up the cry. In the distance he could see them running out from the Rock House, and, as the uproar continued, the kitchen door swung open and a woman stepped boldly out. It was Miz Zoolah, and she would know him by his horse—the stage was set for the play.

He rode up to the store, without glancing at the stone foundation that sheltered Winchester Bassett and three Mormons, and Johnson came tottering out the door. His face was ghastly white and his watery eyes were swimming, but Meshackatee from inside the door was coaching him like a prompter and he stumbled through his part.

"Why, howdy do, Mister Hall," he fawned. "Git down, git down!" And Hall replied in kind. They held a short conversation, then Hall ordered his provisions, and sat watching the Rock House while he waited. There was movement there now and well he knew the glasses that were focused on his form, but he took the matter coolly, tying the provisions on behind, and motioned Johnson to go back to the store. Then he rode off to the north, leaving the leaven to do its work, yet half hoping that Isham would be spared. For when Isham met his fate, Hall wanted to be present—he wanted to launch his black soul into hell, but now he was only the bait of the trap—live bait, to lure the fox from his den.

From his hiding place inside the store Meshackatee watched through his glasses as the outlaws in the Rock House began to swarm, and, when they went for their horses, he relayed the news to Winchester, who was in command of the men behind the wall. Grimes remained in the store, to back up Meshackatee when he called upon the Scarboroughs to surrender, and four men were with the horses, which were hidden behind a hill out of sight from possible raiders. They had learned their parts well, not a man moved or spoke more than to give orders to the terror-stricken Johnson, and, as he tottered wretchedly about, chopping wood and drawing water, they waited like cats by a hole.

An hour passed and Johnson came inside, for Meshackatee distrusted him still, and, as the Scarboroughs milled about without making any start, Grimes took up a grim watch over the storekeeper. He had been seen to make his signals, which he claimed meant all was well, but the Scarboroughs, instead of coming, were gathered in a bunch, apparently engaged in hot argument. Perhaps after all the storekeeper was nervier than he looked, he might even have signaled them a warning, and in that case the posse would find themselves besieged and left in a perilous state. For the first thing that would happen would be the loss of their horses, and along with the horses four men, and to be set afoot in a strange and hostile country was disaster enough in itself. But if these things should happen, Grimes already had the rope that was to hang the treacherous store-keeper.

There was turmoil at the Rock House, men mounted and stepped down again, and finally, after starting in a body for the store, all but two of the gunmen turned back. These two came on at a gallop, spurring and swinging their quirts, and, as they thundered up the trail, Meshackatee focused his glasses and spoke through the doorway to Winchester.

"Here comes Elmo," he said, "and some other crazy fool. Kill the both of them if they go for their guns. But remember, we're deputies! And don't nobody shoot till I say . . . 'Surrender, in the name of the law!' "

He put up his glasses and turned to the storekeeper, who stood like a man in a dream.

"Step out, Mister Johnson," he ordered coldly. "Can't you see them two customers coming?"

"But . . . but you're going to kill them!" protested Johnson in a frenzy.

"Git out there!" Grimes cursed, grabbing him roughly by the neck. "And you stand up to it, or I'll shoot you in the back."

Johnson drew a great breath and stepped out the door just as the horsemen came galloping up. In the lead was Elmo, setting his horse up to make a show, but the man who was behind him reined his horse in more warily, glancing quickly about as he stopped. Meshackatee peeped out through a loophole, nodded his head at Grimes, and stepped to the side of the doorway.

"Who's in there?" demanded Elmo, hearing the quick stir of feet, and Meshackatee threw up his gun.

"Surrender!" he shouted, "in the name of the. . . ."

Bang! went Grimes's rifle, and Elmo lopped forward, shot dead by the heavy .45. The man behind made a grab for his carbine, then whirled his horse to flee, but before he could start, there was a volley from the foundation and he pitched off, still clutching at his gun. The horse raced away, pitching and kicking at the saddle gun, which hung flopping, half drawn from the scabbard, and this was the messenger of defeat for the Scarboroughs—another empty saddle coming home. They who lived by the sword had perished by the sword—the ambushers had run into an ambush. And in this last disaster Isham Scarborough read his doom. When the morning came again, he was gone.

CHAPTER TWENTY-SIX

The Scarborough gang disappeared overnight, disappeared and was lost track of completely, and its dissolution was as complete as that of a bubble that suddenly explodes and is gone. The outlaws and horse thieves who had so terrorized the country, carrying their trade as far as Wyoming and Texas, took to the hills and were gone, leaving the stock they had stolen to be rounded up and restored by Meshackatee. In the corrals by the Rock House horses and cattle awaited their owners, and the Rock House itself, once the hold-out of the gang, became the abode of Tonto County deputies. But Isham himself, the wolf who had turned fox, was lost and could not be found.

He had started west, taking the trail to Geronimo, and somewhere on the way he had disappeared. For hundreds of miles along the base of the Mogollon Rim, and for thousands of square miles along its top, there was a forest of pines as unbroken as the first wilderness, as untracked as the Arctic regions. Once out of the trail a man was lost to all pursuit but, knowing his directions, he was free to ride on as he pleased until he came to the edge of the forest. Into this covert of trees and brush Isham had slipped like a weasel, leaving his wife to ride on to Geronimo, but Hall cut his trail at last, and, after a month of hard riding, he, too, rode into Geronimo. For the wolf, now turned fox, had doubled on his tracks and taken shelter within the shadow of the law.

There had been a time when Isham had scoffed at the law,

but that was in Tonto County. Geronimo County was different, and there was also a sharp rivalry between the mountain and valley counties. Geronimo was down in the valley, a land of heat and broad canals and alfalfa fields stretching away for miles, and its people were peaceably inclined, but the mountainous Tonto had achieved an unenviable reputation as the home of horse thieves and outlaws. The Geronimo papers had made the most of his outlawry but Isham had reckoned well when he depended upon local jealousy to protect him from the hand of the law. No Tonto County deputy could arrest him in Geronimo, and he knew that no Geronimo deputy would. And to add to his security it soon became evident that Tonto was glad to get rid of him. The county was bankrupt already from trying to convict him and it was content to let sleeping dogs lie.

This much Hall learned before he had been in town an hour—and then he experienced a shock. A tall man that he knew sauntered into the saloon and regarded him out of the tail of his eye—it was Burge Masters, one of the Scarborough gunmen. He took a drink and sauntered out, and, as Hall sat at a card table, another tall Texan walked in.

"Say," he said, coming over to where Hall sat, "haven't I seen you before around here somewhere?"

"Why, not that I know of," responded Hall, and looked him over carefully. He belonged to a breed that he knew all too well—heavy-jawed with high cheek bones and narrowed eyes—he was a gunman, straight from Texas. But what was he doing here in this peaceful farming community? The answer was in his eyes. He was there for a purpose and that purpose, for some reason, was not unconnected with Hall.

"That your horse out there?" inquired the Texan abruptly, "blue roan with a slit in one ear? Well, I'll have you know you stole 'im!"

He struck the table and Hall glanced up at him quickly, but

he did not make a move.

"You are mistaken, my friend," he answered at last, and the Texan turned away. Hall stepped out the door after him, just in time to see three Texans making a critical examination of his roan. And then it flashed over him, the old Scarborough trick that Isham had attempted at Cold Spring. They were trying to prove him a horse thief. He stood and watched them, stamping their faces on his memory, and at last they slouched away. But he had the answer now—they were still Scarborough gunmen, and they knew he had come with a purpose. What that purpose was he would admit to no man, but they knew, and Isham would know. He was there to kill the last of the Scarboroughs.

Even if he were not superstitious, the appearance of Hall McIvor would send the chill of fear over Isham, for the blue roan that he rode had lured Red to his death, and then horse and man had lured Elmo. It was like the shadow of a raven, the heavy winging of death itself, to see that drooping roan at the horse rack, and, as Hall watched the street, he was conscious of tense faces that seemed to divine his mission. Perhaps it was his clothes, torn by riding through the brush, or the stern set look in his eyes, but he could tell by their looks that these strangers knew all about him, although now they studiously ignored him. Even the Texans kept away from him, retreating to the saloon across the street, but he knew what was in their hearts. There was a $1,000 reward on his head.

Not for nothing had Burge Masters's friend slapped the table insultingly and accused him of being a horse thief; they were out for the reward, and, if he refused to fight, there were other ways of embroiling him. Hall sensed mischief in the air and yet he was puzzled—they seemed to be prepared for his coming. Where before there had been one Texan, now there were eight or ten, all armed and watching him closely, and, as he mounted his tired horse and rode him down to the corral, he saw two of them swing up and start after him. Then he knew it—he had ridden into a trap. Isham had assembled his gunmen and made all things ready, and then let his presence be known, and Hall, following blindly, had ridden into an ambush, right there in that peaceful farming town. If he fled, they would follow him, and if he stayed—well, then it would be ten to one.

He rode down to the feed corral and looked it over closely, then summoned the proprietor from his office.

"Put this horse in a box stall," he directed, "and don't let any person go near him. I want to leave him saddled, and I'll hold you personally responsible if he isn't right here when I want him."

"All right, pardner," answered the livery stable keeper, "I suppose the horse is yours?"

"Yes, and here's the bill of sale."

Hall took out the bill of sale that he had carefully preserved and showed it to the worldly-wise proprietor, who nodded and passed it back.

"Kee-reck," he remarked. " 'Be sure you're right,' sez I, 'and then go ahead.' Your horse will be here when you call for him."

The Texans had disappeared when Hall returned to the main street, but he sat with his back to the wall. It was a habit he had acquired in just such towns as this, when the clans had gathered for court day. But here all was different, the air was furnace hot and strange birds fluttered about through the palms; there was the smell of desert greasewood, the rank tang of arrow weed, and the fragrance of sun-ripened hay. Heavy wagons dragged past, loaded with wheat for the flour mill that stood at the edge of the river bottom; long-haired Indians strode by, their bare feet whispering along the sidewalk, and Mexicans sat on their heels, smoking. There were ranchers in sweaty shirts and faded-out overalls, and the usual collection of bums, but the Texans were gone, and, as evening came on, Hall retired to his room above the saloon.

Here was a new problem, new conditions, a conspiracy on foot to draw him into a quarrel, and he wondered rather wearily if it would not be better to withdraw and come in again. Isham Scarborough had rented a ranch several miles out of town and was reported to be harvesting his wheat; he was forewarned now, and, if Hall rode to his ranch, he would expose his hand to no purpose. And then the hired gunmen, who even now were dogging his footsteps, would find the opportunity they sought. He would be shot down from ambush, somewhere along the road, and Isham would escape unscathed. Every circumstance was against him, but now he could not flee, for they would hunt him down like a rabbit. All he could do was to stand pat and wait.

In towns like Geronimo there is but one place to wait and Hall found himself back in the saloon. The Keno was the largest by far in the city and there he would find company and friends. It was a protection, in a way, to mingle with the crowd that gathered to gamble and drink, and, if the Texans came to gang him, these men of the valley would see that he had fair play. So as the evening came on, making the darkened streets danger-ous, he drifted back into the Keno, and to pass away the time he ventured small sums at roulette, always keeping one eye on the door. And then they came in, not eight or ten of them, but fifteen or twenty armed Texans, and a hush settled over the room.

The skitter of the roulette ball sounded with painful distinct-ness, and drunken men, wrangling in an uproar, heard their voices break through and rise high in the sudden silence. Texans were rare in Geronimo, they almost never came there, and especially in the heat of summer, and these swashbucklers from Tonto were known for what they were, although their purpose that night was still a mystery. All the Arizonians knew was that they were out to make trouble—Hall knew they had come to get him. They called for drinks and then scattered through the room, some watching the crap games, others losing a dollar at roulette, but gradually closing in. A hand, coming from nowhere, reached out to steal his pistol; another man jostled him from behind, but, as the gang surged toward him, Hall slipped between two tables and stood with his back to the wall.

There was a pause, in which crap dealers slid down softly beneath their tables and the rest of the assembly stood frozen, and then Hall spoke to the nearest of the gang.

"What can I do for you, my friend?" he asked with deceptive quietness, and the nerve of the Texan broke.

"Have a drink!" He guffawed, turning and heading for the bar, but Burge Masters stepped out in his place.

"We want you," he said, "and you might as well come quietly. If you don't. . . ."

"I won't come," stated Hall.

There was another pause, and the crowd by the door suddenly ducked and charged out into the street, then, after an interval, another crowd surged in, and in the lead strode Wahoo Meshackatee. He had a gun in each hand, and, when he saw the Texans, he started, then glanced inquiringly at Hall.

"Well, hello," he exclaimed, "what's going on here, anyhow? Have I broke in on a little family party?"

Burge Masters turned his head but he did not speak and his men began to shuffle away.

"Oh, nothing much," he mumbled, and Meshackatee beckoned to Hall, then held up his hand to the barkeeper.

"Have a drink, boys," he said. "Your faces seem familiar. Long time since I've seen a live Texan."

They looked at him and winced, for they knew what he meant, and suddenly all the fight went out of them.

"Well," grumbled Masters, and they drank in stony silence, then turned and filed out of the door.

CHAPTER TWENTY-SEVEN

"What you doing down here?" demanded Meshackatee of Hall as soon as he could draw him aside. "And what was that . . . a horse thieves' reunion?"

"Those are Scarborough gunmen," answered Hall quietly. "We're lucky to get off alive."

"You're lucky," corrected Meshackatee. "But, say, have you seen Winchester? The rascal is down here somewhere."

"Let's find him," declared Hall, and started for the door, but Meshackatee drew him back.

"Keep inside," he advised. "Them *Tejanos* will pot you if you show yourself in the door. Leave 'im alone. I ain't worried about Winchester."

"But this town is dangerous," protested Hall. "We three ought to get together. I believe there's a reward . . . and a big one, too . . . on the head of every one of us."

"Come over here in the corner," beckoned Meshackatee, and they took seats at a table in the rear. "Now, listen," he said, "we stay here all night. You're dead right . . . the damned burg is dangerous. These officers in town, the city marshal and such, have crept plumb under the house. It's Texas Day . . . or was. But here's the hell of it. I've got it straight enough, they're jest waiting for one of us to leave. We're safe, here in town, but the minute we leave . . . well, I'm thinking about writing my will."

"I can't understand it," returned Hall, "and yet, in a way, I can. Miz Zoolah came ahead and hired all these gunmen, and then Isham broke cover and joined her. He's got a ranch out here somewhere. . . ."

"That's where Winchester is," whispered Meshackatee. "They don't know he's come down. He's out looking over the ground."

"Just where is this ranch?" asked Hall after a pause, and, when Meshackatee told him, he fell silent. The night dragged on slowly and the games of chance closed; they watched and slept by turns, but, as the morning drew near, Hall rose up quietly and slipped out by the back way to the corral. In the box stall he found his horse and led him quickly to the street, then mounted and rode off through the darkness. Something told him to go back, to turn and ride for the hills, to seek out Allifair and never come back, but something else urged him on, something warned him to strike now, before his enemies could kill him by treachery. In the river bottom silt his horse's hoofs were muffled; he threaded the ghostly roadways in silence, and at the fourth crossroad south he turned to the west, taking shelter beneath the blackness of tall cottonwoods.

It was the darkness before the dawn when he sighted the place and knew it by the baying of hounds, and, finding some wasteland nearby covered with mesquite trees and high weeds, he took cover and waited for the light. But now that he was still, his heart grew sick and he almost repented of his purpose. A little more patience, a few more days of grace, and Meshackatee or Winchester might kill Isham. But, no, that was wrong, for even in one day Isham's gunmen might shoot down all three of them. The time to strike was now, before they had recovered from their surprise and had a chance to lay other plans, and the man to strike was Isham, the head and front of the gang, the man whose cunning and hate urged them on. Three times already Hall had set out to kill him and each time had been diverted from his purpose. This time he would die if he failed.

As the sun came up, he crept to the edge of the wild land

and searched the Scarborough ranch with his glasses, and already they were astir, loading some wheat sacks on a hay wagon, rearranging them, making a trench down the middle. He lay watching them curiously, trying to divine their zealous interest in the loading of that grist for the mill, but when the horses were hitched up, he was suddenly enlightened, for Isham climbed up on the load. It was a traveling fort, a barricade on wheels, and, as he settled down and took the reins, they handed him up his guns and opened the gate to the road. Men that Hall had not seen now appeared from their ambush, hurrying to catch up their mounts and follow, and, while they were saddling, Isham drove out the gate and turned his team toward town.

Hall drew back from his look-out and ran to his horse, then hurried to a place by the road, but, as the wagon came toward him, he could see nothing but Isham's feet—he was concealed behind a wall of solid wheat. He hesitated, for there were loopholes between the piled-up sacks and Isham would have him at his mercy, and yet, if he allowed this chance to slip by. . . . He crouched back, confused and distrait. But while he weighed the chances against him, there was a stir across the road, a rush and a breaking of brush, and from the cover of the mesquite thicket a horseman burst out and went charging down on the wagon. Isham rose up to scramble back, but the horseman was upon him. He fired twice, never slackening his pace, and then, without a pause, he reined back into the brush and went plunging away through the trees. Hall drew back trembling—it was Winchester Bassett, and whoever knew Winchester to miss?

At the shooting the heavy farm team shied and cramped the wheels, but now with reins dangling they went galloping up the road, spilling off grain sacks in their terrified flight. There was a yell from the ranch house, the *patter* of pursuing hoof beats, and, as the Texans dashed past, Hall ran for his horse and was lost in the thicket of mesquites. Isham Scarborough was dead and Winchester had killed him, but there was still the law to be reckoned with. There would be a search for the murderer, a hue and cry through the wastelands, perhaps later a marking down of tracks, and, while Winchester had fired the shots, it would go hard with Hall if he were caught near the scene of the crime. Winchester had counted his life as nothing, charging out like a whirlwind and winning by his very audacity, but now he would flee as swiftly as he had come, leaving nothing but his horse tracks by the road. Hall spurred through the thickets and came out on a section line, but, as he was about to take flight, he paused.

Back in the corner of the Keno, watched over only by his dog, the big-hearted Meshackatee was sleeping across the table, unsuspecting of the storm about to burst. In their rage at Isham's death, the Texans might shoot him down, or have the officers take him in charge, and the devilish spite of Miz Zoolah was still to be reckoned with—she, too, might hire him killed for revenge. Hall turned his horse toward town and went galloping up a side street just as the first Texans, riding alongside the wagon, came shouting the news up the street. There was a rush of curious people and the saloon was deserted when Hall burst in through the back door. Even the barkeepers were gone, and Meshackatee had gone with them—Hall stepped to the swinging doors.

The wagon had stopped in the middle of the street and the people were swarming around it, and up on the broad platform, now cleared of its wheat, Miz Zoolah was standing above Isham.

"He's dead," she announced, as men scrambled to lift the body. "Leave 'im alone, I tell ye, he's dead. But I know who killed him, and, if there's an ounce of manhood in any of you,

185

you'll ride till you ketch Hall McIvor. He's riding a blue roan and. . . ."

Hall ducked through the door and made a run out the back way, but, as he mounted, he took a second thought. He had not killed Isham Scarborough, and it could not be proved—there was no one to stand witness against him—but if he fled for the hills and was pursued and brought back, the fact would be used against him. And if the Texans led the posse, as they undoubtedly would, it would end in a fight to the death. He reined his horse back and rode straight to the courthouse, where he gave himself up to the sheriff.

CHAPTER TWENTY-EIGHT

Isham Scarborough was dead but the Scarborough gang still lived, and soon what had long been suspected was proven—Miz Zoolah had been its brains. Isham had put up the bluff, the loud talk, and the rough work, but she had done the thinking that had directed his coarse violence along the ways of destruction and death. And, since she was its head, the gang still lived on, to carry out her will to the end. She it was who had laid the man trap at Geronimo, to net the last of her husband's enemies, and, although Hall was in jail and so safe from open violence, even there he felt the breath of her hatred. She appeared at his cell door, to identify him positively before she swore out a warrant against him, and the look in her pale eyes was as baleful as a rattlesnake's when it raises its head to strike.

"That's the man," she said, "I'd swear to him anywhere. He's the man that killed my husband."

And before the Justice of the Peace, when he was arraigned for examination, she accused him with passionate hate.

"He's a McIvor!" she cried. "His father killed my brother and my elder sister's son! And now he's killed my husband . . . he shot him from ambush, but I reached him before he died. He had fallen from the wagon, and, when I raised his head, he whispered . . . 'Hall killed me . . . Hall McIvor!' And then he fell back, dead."

That was all her testimony, the only thing that held him and the one thing that could not be shaken, and he was bound over to the Grand Jury, which held him for trial at the pending session of court. But had Isham spoken these words before he died? In the dreary days that followed Hall debated it, pro and con, but he knew and she knew that, as long as she swore to it, it might as well be the fact. For Isham was dead, there were no other witnesses, and it was a question of veracity between Miz Zoolah and himself, with the odds in favor of the woman. He was shut up in a cell, without a single friend to consult with or to carry a message to Allifair, but she was at large, with a band of Texas gunmen to see that his friends did not come.

Meshackatee could help him, but Hall knew in his heart that Meshackatee dared not come; the man trap was still set, and he would not escape again as he had when he first came to town. And Allifair could help, for she had heard Isham's threats and his offer of a reward for his death, but the moment she appeared, her aunt would seize upon her and make her a virtual prisoner. Winchester Bassett could help most, if he happened to be so minded, but he had escaped to the hills, riding a relay of swift horses, and established a perfect alibi. On the very day of the killing he had been seen in Maverick Basin, a hundred and twenty miles away. So the whole matter stood and Hall waited in silence until the day of his trial came at last.

A thousand times, as he lay sweltering in the heat, breathing the dead, sickly air of his prison, he thought of Allifair, hidden away in their eagles' nest and watching the empty trail. How many times as the two long months dragged by must she have thought he was wounded or killed, and yet there was no one but Meshackatee that he would trust with a message, for Miz Zoolah was still on the watch. Somewhere, she knew, Hall had hidden away Allifair, and she had her spies even in the jail, and rather than expose her to the wrath of the Randolphs, Hall left Allifair to wait on alone. How she would live he could only guess, for her supplies would be exhausted, but he imagined her at dawn gathering grass seeds and piñon nuts or bringing back turkeys from her traps. He imagined her roasting acorns to grind them up for coffee and ranging like a quail to find berries, even gnawing the bark of trees or cooking mescal heads to break the dead monotony of her diet. Yet even that was better, he said in his heart, than to fall into the clutches of Miz Zoolah.

He went to his trial like a man in a dream following the sheriff up the narrow winding stairs, but when he entered the crowded courtroom with its bank of auditors standing behind, he swept the sea of faces with keen eyes. Here were the men that were to try him, the men of Geronimo, for what they thought would be reflected in the jury that would be called to hear his case. The jury would cast the ballot, but The People would decide, for thought is as fluid as air. It passes from man to man despite the menace of bailiffs and the charges of the court commanding silence, and the opinion of the majority finds its expression at last when the foreman says: "Guilty" or "Not Guilty."

Hall pleaded "Not Guilty," and he pleaded according to fact, for his hand was innocent of the crime, yet so intimate is the connection between what we think and what we are that somehow he felt himself the killer. He had come to Geronimo to kill Isham or be killed; he had ridden to his ranch to waylay him, and only the intervention of Winchester Bassett had kept him from accomplishing his purpose. Not that he held himself to blame, for the teachings of a lifetime made him consider such an act as praiseworthy, but the look in his eyes was that of a man-killer who seeks no excuse for his crime. And the men of Geronimo, being a hardy band of citizens, looked on in grim approval. According to their code he had committed no crime—he had fought a fair fight and won.

Being questioned, he admitted that on the morning of the killing he had been present at the scene of the crime; he acknowledged his connection with the Maverick Basin war and his grudge against the deceased, but he denied most vigorously that he had fired the shots that had resulted in the death of Isham. All this he did voluntarily, in the form of a statement, and then he sat down and waited. There was a stir in the crowd and Mrs. Scarborough stepped forward, swathed in black to emphasize her widowhood, but when she began to talk, she threw back the long veil and her eyes became set with hate. Question after question was asked and answered, the time and place were fully established, and then the district attorney asked the one crucial question:

"And what did your husband say?"

"He said," she declared passionately, " 'Hall killed me . . . Hall McIvor!' "

And then she turned and looked at him.

"That is all," announced the district attorney, and rested his case, at which there was another stir in the crowd. Hall turned with the rest, and, when he saw Meshackatee's huge head, his broad shoulders, and curling black beard, he smiled for the first time that day.

"I call that man for my witness," he said to the judge, but there was another surprise in store for him. Following close behind Meshackatee and concealed by his great bulk came Allifair Randolph, smiling. He sprang up to meet her, but the bailiff snatched him back, the district attorney shouted out some protest, and then, still held apart, they gave greeting with their eyes while the crowd rose up and gaped. Here was the woman in the case, the woman we always look for, the one we are directed to find, and, when she stepped into the witness box, her face radiant with love, the jury gazed about in wonder. But when they saw the glare in the eyes of Mrs. Scarborough, they read the whole story at a glance. This case that they were trying was not a plain killing, it was battle between women as well, and, when women are involved, as the jury knew full well, the facts are often thrown to the winds. Even the sanctity of the oath is lightly disregarded and passion pulls down reason from its throne, and so they leaned forward to listen with open mind, as the judge had so carefully instructed them.

Allifair, being questioned, explained the feud behind a feud— the Randolph-McIvor war and its relation to the battle that had ended in the death of Isham. Hall's lawyer repeated the questions as Hall whispered them into his ear, and, after she had told of the opposition to their marriage, the lawyer suddenly saw a way out.

"And do I understand," he asked, "that the complaining witness, Missus Scarborough, is a member of the Randolph clan? Well, please inform the jury if at any time, to your knowledge, she threatened the life of the defendant."

"Yes," answered Allifair. "One night he came to meet me, and, while we were talking, my aunt crept up behind us and threatened to shoot him with a pistol. And when I interfered, she said she would kill me before she would let me marry a McIvor."

"And do you consider that this prejudice, this clan feeling as a Randolph, would render it impossible for your aunt to give fair testimony where the life of the defendant was at stake?"

"I object!" spoke up the district attorney, but the judge overruled him, and Allifair answered the question.

"I believe she would say anything, or do anything," she replied, "that would keep us from being married."

"That is all," said the lawyer, and summoned Meshackatee, but before he took the stand, Meshackatee whispered to the bailiff, who turned and looked sharply into the audience.

"Your honor," began Meshackatee, as the bailiff seemed to hesitate, "I have reason to believe that a band of armed men have come into court here to kill me. I refer particularly to that bunch of bad Texans."

He jerked his thumb in the direction of the front seats where the Scarborough gunmen under the direction of Burge Masters sat glaring with narrowed eyes.

"Search the gentlemen," ordered the judge, "and, while you are about it, remove that pistol from the witness."

The bailiff rapped for silence and the judge went on sternly. "At the first sign of disturbance I will order the courtroom cleared. Any who wish may now leave the room."

The gunmen rose up, drawing their coats over their pistols, and filed sullenly out of court.

"Thank you, Judge." Meshackatee bowed, turning his belt over to the bailiff, and he stepped ponderously up into the witness chair.

"I am a deputy sheriff of Tonto County," he replied to the lawyer's first question. "Yes, I know the defendant well. He served as a deputy during the Maverick Basin trouble, and is a gentleman of the highest integrity. Yes, I have often heard him say that he disapproved of all feuds and especially of the Randolph-McIvor war. His sole object, so he informed me, in entering Maverick Basin was to rescue and marry Miss Randolph. She was being held, practically as a prisoner, by Missus Scarborough."

Hall's lawyer was beginning to beam, the jury exchanged glances, and, as Meshackatee went on to show Miz Zoolah's prejudice against McIvor, she rose up and left the room. Allifair nodded to Hall and smiled, even the judge began to unbend, but as he was making a ruling, Hall sprang to his feet and pointed toward the door.

"Your Honor!" he cried, "I want that woman restrained. I have reason to believe. . . ."

"Sit down!" ordered the judge, and, as Hall obeyed, Mrs. Scarborough came swiftly down the aisle. Her face was half concealed beneath the veil of heavy crêpe that hung from her widow's bonnet, but her right hand was hidden beneath the folds of a black shawl that she had thrown about her shoulders. And something about her step as she came down toward him warned Hall of the murder in her heart.

"This is not Kentucky," went on the judge severely, "nor is it Maverick Basin. You are safe in the custody of the court."

Hall rose up again and glanced helplessly about, then dropped his hands by his side.

"Very well," he replied, and, as Mrs. Scarborough swept by him, he turned and met her eye. "I have never struck a woman yet," he said, and her thin lips parted in a sneer.

"No," she answered, and, while they gazed at her fascinated, she whipped out a pistol, full-cocked. "I'll show you!" she cried, and, pressing it against his breast, she gave the trigger a jerk. But the gun only snapped, for her widow's veil, hanging down from her bonnet, had caught on the hammer and fouled it. She struggled to release it, to cock and fire again, and Hall turned his eyes on the judge.

"And I never will," he added, "not even to save my life."

"Seize that woman!" shouted the judge, suddenly roused from the paralysis that had frozen every man in his place, but the bailiff had come to life first. He struck the gun to one side and crushed Miz Zoolah's arms to her sides, and, as she fought like a wildcat, others rushed in to help him, while the crowd stampeded through the doors.

"I'll git you!" she shrieked, her pale eyes blazing with rage as Hall McIvor stood smiling before her—but his smile was not for her. Allifair had stood fast and now she came running to throw herself into his arms.

"God has saved you," she sobbed, and he bowed his head.

"Yes," he said. "Saved me for you."

They stood locked in each other's arms, oblivious of the spectators, unconscious of what was going on, and, when they looked about, the clerk was piling up his books and the district attorney was speaking.

"If the court please," he said, "the conduct of the complaining witness has destroyed the value, in my opinion, of her testimony, and I therefore ask the court to direct an acquittal, since no jury would convict on such evidence."

As court was adjourned, he came over and shook hands, wishing them all the happiness in life, and Hall and Allifair were still receiving congratulations when Meshackatee came hurrying back.

"Well, come on, come on," he boomed, "we've got her locked up in jail! And I'll say right now she's half red and the other half stinging scorpion. So if you're going to git married, you'd better do it quick, before she breaks down the bars. I'll give the bride away, if you'll excuse these clothes, but, by grab, if them scoundrels hadn't jinglebobbed my ears, I'd've stole Miss Allifair myself. A prettier woman . . . or a braver woman, either . . . I never expect to see. She lived up in them cliff-dwellings for nigh onto two months, and, when I come by there. . . . Well, I'll go and git the license. There's the judge there, trying to flag you."

The judge indeed was beckoning them to his chambers, and, when they had entered, he gave Hall his hand while Allifair looked on, smiling.

"Mister McIvor," he said, "I owe you an apology. And allow me to retract what I said about Kentucky, a state that may well be proud of you. Whatever she may lack in respect for the law, you have learned there a chivalry and a reverence for womankind that I never expected to witness. If you and Miss Randolph will do me the honor, I shall be happy to officiate at your marriage."

Hall hesitated a moment and glanced down at Allifair, who blushed and nodded her head.

"We thank you, Judge," he said, "and, since you have referred to Kentucky, let me say that our marriage will end the greatest feud that has ever existed in that state. The Randolphs and McIvors have fought for twenty years, and our code may seem different from yours, but despite our lawless acts we McIvors love truth and justice and hold our honor above our lives."

"You have shown," declared the judge, "that that is no idle phrase. I can see that it comes from your heart. But why, if I may ask, did you refuse to strike that woman? Would you stand there and allow her to kill you?"

"No gentleman . . . ," began Hall, and then he stopped and met Allifair's unbelieving gaze. "She was a Randolph," he said, and bowed.

"Oh, Hall," reproached Allifair, suddenly clutching at his hand, and then her eyes softened and she smiled.

"The Randolphs love honor, too," she said. "They will learn to forgive us . . . now."

ACKNOWLEDGMENTS

"Maverick Basin" by Dane Coolidge first appeared as a three-part serial in *The Popular Magazine* (7/7/20–8/7/20). Copyright © 1920 by Street & Smith Publications, Inc. Copyright © renewed 1948 by Nancy Roberts Collins. Acknowledgment is made to Condé Nast Publications, Inc., for their co-operation. Copyright © 2009 by Golden West Literary Agency for restored material.

ABOUT THE AUTHOR

Dane Coolidge was born in Natick, Massachusetts. He moved early to northern California with his family and was graduated from Stanford University in 1898. In his summers he worked as a field collector and in 1896 was employed by the British Museum in this capacity in northern Mexico. Coolidge's background as a naturalist is a trademark in his Western fiction along with his personal familiarity with the vast, isolated regions of the American West and its deserts—especially Death Valley. Coolidge married Mary Roberts, a feminist and a professor of sociology at Mills College, in 1906. In the summers, these two ventured among the Indian nations and together they co-authored non-fiction books about the Navajos and the Seris. *Hidden Water* (1910), Coolidge's first Western novel, marked the beginning of a career that saw many of his novels serialized in magazines prior to book publication. There is an extraordinary breadth in these novels from *Wunpost* (1920) set in Death Valley to *Maverick Makers* (1931), a Texas Rangers story. Many of his novels are concerned with prospecting and mining from *Shadow Mountain* (1920) and *Lost Wagons* (1923) based on actual historical episodes in the mining history of Death Valley to a fictional treatment of Colonel Bill Greene's discovery of the fabulous Capote copper mine in Mexico, a central theme in *Wolf's Candle* (1935) and *Rawhide Johnny* (1936). *The New York Times Book Review* commented on *Hell's Hip Pocket* (1939) that "no other man in the field today writes better Western tales than Dane Coolidge." Coolidge, who died in 1940, wrote with a definite grace and leisurely pace all but lost to the Western story after the Second World War, although Nelson C. Nye, an admirer of Coolidge, tried in his own fiction to capture this same ambiance. The attention to the land and accurate detail make a Dane Coolidge Western story rewarding to readers of any generation. *Riders of Deseret* will be his next Five Star Western.